THE BIG BOW MYSTERY
&
THE MURDERS IN THE RUE MORGUE

'THE DETECTIVE STORY CLUB is a clearing house for the best detective and mystery stories chosen for you by a select committee of experts. Only the most ingenious crime stories will be published under the THE DETECTIVE STORY CLUB imprint. A special distinguishing stamp appears on the wrapper and title page of every THE DETECTIVE STORY CLUB book—the Man with the Gun. Always look for the Man with the Gun when buying a Crime book.'

Wm. Collins Sons & Co. Ltd., 1929

Now the Man with the Gun is back in this series of COLLINS CRIME CLUB reprints, and with him the chance to experience the classic books that influenced the Golden Age of crime fiction.

THE DETECTIVE STORY CLUB

THE BIG BOW MYSTERY

(THE PERFECT CRIME)

A STORY OF CRIME BY

ISRAEL ZANGWILL

&

THE MURDERS IN THE RUE MORGUE
BY EDGAR ALLAN POE

WITH AN INTRODUCTION BY
JOHN CURRAN

COLLINS
CRIME
CLUB

COLLINS CRIME CLUB
An imprint of HarperCollins*Publishers*
1 London Bridge Street
London SE1 9GF
www.harpercollins.co.uk

This edition 2015
1

First published in Great Britain as *The Big Bow Mystery*
by Henry & Co. 1892
Published as *The Perfect Crime* by The Detective Story Club Ltd
for Wm Collins Sons & Co. Ltd 1929
'The Murders in the Rue Morgue'
first published by Graham's Magazine 1841

A catalogue record for this book is
available from the British Library

ISBN 978-0-00-813728-1

Printed and bound in Great Britain by
Clays Ltd, St Ives plc

INTRODUCTION

WHEN a corpse is found, with its throat cut and no sign of a weapon, in a room locked and bolted from the inside, both murder and suicide must be discarded as impossible. But writers of detective fiction, and their readers, are more circumspect. For them these fascinating conditions pose the questions: *Whodunit?* and, even more intriguingly, *How?*

Edgar Allan Poe's 'The Murders in the Rue Morgue' (1841) was not only the first detective story, but also the first locked-room detective story; and *The Big Bow Mystery* (1892) by Israel Zangwill (1864–1926) was the first book-length example of the form. As such, it occupies an important place in the history of detective fiction.

The story first appeared in 1891 as a serial in the London daily *Star* newspaper, for which Zangwill worked at the time; it was published in book form the following year and collected in Zangwill's *The Grey Wig: Stories and Novelettes* in 1903. In a preface, written for an 1895 edition of his book, the author perceptively acknowledged what is, in essence, the 'fair-play' rule of detective fiction (as adopted many years later by the Detection Club) when he wrote:

> 'The indispensable condition of a good mystery is that it should be able and unable to be solved by the reader, and that that the writer's solution should satisfy. And not only must the solution be adequate, but all its data must be given in the body of the story.'

Zangwill had long suspected, he explained, that 'no mystery-monger had ever murdered a man in a room to which there was no possible access' and that, although he had devised such a solution, it lay dormant until the editor of 'a popular London evening newspaper' asked him 'to provide . . . a more original piece of fiction'. As the story unfolded—written in a fortnight 'day by day', according to the author—readers of the serial submitted 'unsolicited testimonials in the shape of solutions', although they 'had failed, one and all, to hit on the real murderer'. (One can't help wondering if the variety of possible solutions put forward in the course of the novel were some of these suggestions.)

The previous quarter-century had seen the publication of landmark novels of detective fiction: Wilkie Collins's *The Moonstone* (1868), Charles Dickens's *The Mystery of Edwin Drood* (1870), Anna Katharine Green's *The Leavenworth Case* (1878). And in the years immediately preceding *The Big Bow Mystery* the appearance of the world's first 'consulting detective', Sherlock Holmes, ushered in the pre-Golden Age of detective fiction. Two of Holmes's full-length investigations—*A Study in Scarlet* (1888) and *The Sign of (the) Four* (1890)—were followed by the first dozen of the phenomenally successful short stories in the *Strand* magazine, beginning in July 1891 with 'A Scandal in Bohemia'. So when Zangwill's novel was published, the public appetite for crime fiction was well established—and almost insatiable.

Zangwill, the son of Latvian and Polish immigrants, was born in London's East End and showed literary promise as early as eighteen. A teacher for some years after he graduated from London University, he eventually left the profession to write full-time, publishing hundreds of essays, as well as novels, short stories and plays produced in London and New York. His work concentrated on political, social and Jewish issues but *The Big Bow Mystery* was his only venture into detective fiction.

Given this background, his novel is more socially aware than many of its contemporaries. Two of the main characters are closely involved with the labour movement and a detailed picture of the social conditions of London's East

End and its denizens is conveyed through the characters and their circumstances. Dickensian names—the upright Arthur Constant, the hugely entertaining Mrs Drabdump, the enigmatic Edward Wimp, the elusive Jessie Dymond and the wonderfully named Denzil Cantercot—help to reinforce this milieu. A less than flattering picture of the police, and their initial attempts to solve the case, against a background of 'a frigid grey mist' and 'cold [that] cut like a many-bladed knife' contribute to the overall mood of a powerless stratum of society.

In the course of the novel the reader is treated to a baffling murder, an investigation, an inquest, a checking of alibis, a court case, a last-minute revelation and a shocking denouement; in fact, most of the components of the best detective fiction. And throughout, the locked room problem shares centre-stage with the 'whodunit' element. A nod to Poe in Chapter IV and the somewhat similar problem presented to his detective and readers in 'The Murders in the Rue Morgue' is inevitable; although rest assured that while the problem in both stories may be similar, Zangwill's solution is totally different. Arguably it is superior, because, like all clever solutions, it contains elements of the psychological as well as the physical; as the villain confidently asserts in the closing pages, 'to dash a half-truth in the world's eyes is the surest way of blinding it altogether'. The explanation of the riddle is, in retrospect, tantalisingly simple and maddeningly obvious and, as with many such problems, if you can discern the 'how', you automatically know the 'who'. Variations on the solution have been adapted and adopted many times since; and by some of the most resourceful practitioners in the genre.

Perhaps because 'the solution of the inexplicable problem agitated mankind from China to Peru' and had been 'discussed in every language under the sun', the novel features, in the closing chapters, the (unnamed) Home Secretary, as well as a guest appearance by William Gladstone. Zangwill writes in a prefatory Note that the justification for introducing the then Prime Minister 'into a fictitious scene is defended on the grounds that he is largely mythical'.

Within a decade of Zangwill's novel, Sherlock Holmes returned, miraculously, from the Reichenbach Falls, Chesterton's immortal Father Brown and Freeman's famous Dr Thorndyke began their careers in 'The Blue Cross' (1903) and *The Red Thumb Mark* (1907) respectively; and the world of crime fiction was never the same again.

The Big Bow Mystery was filmed in a semi-silent version as *The Perfect Crime* in 1928 and as *The Verdict* in 1946. With the former very much in the public consciousness when Collins began The Detective Story Club imprint in July 1929, Zangwill's book was an obvious choice as one of the launch titles, and explains the change of title on the jacket, even though it was still entitled *The Big Bow Mystery* inside.

DR JOHN CURRAN
Dublin, March 2015

THE BIG BOW MYSTERY

BY

ISRAEL ZANGWILL

NOTE

THE Mystery which the author will always associate with this story is how he got through the task of writing it. It was written in a fortnight—day by day—to meet a sudden demand from the *Star*, which made 'a new departure' with it.

The said fortnight was further disturbed by an extraordinary combined attack of other troubles and tasks. This is no excuse for the shortcomings of the book, as it was always open to the writer to revise or suppress it. The latter function may safely be left to the public, while if the work stands—almost to a letter—as it appeared in the *Star*, it is because the author cannot tell a story more than once.

The introduction of Mr Gladstone into a fictitious scene is defended on the ground that he is largely mythical.

I. Z.

PREFACE

As this little book was written some four years ago, I feel able to review it without prejudice. A new book just hot from the brain is naturally apt to appear faulty to its begetter, but an old book has got into the proper perspective and may be praised by him without fear or favour. *The Big Bow Mystery* seems to me an excellent murder story, as murder stories go, for, while as sensational as the most of them, it contains more humour and character creation than the best. Indeed, the humour is too abundant. Mysteries should be sedate and sober. There should be a pervasive atmosphere of horror and awe such as Poe manages to create. Humour is out of tone; it would be more artistic to preserve a sombre note throughout. But I was a realist in those days, and in real life mysteries occur to real persons with their individual humours, and mysterious circumstances are apt to be complicated by comic. The indispensable condition of a good mystery is that it should be able and unable to be solved by the reader, and that the writer's solution should satisfy. Many a mystery runs on breathlessly enough till the *dénouement* is reached, only to leave the reader with the sense of having been robbed of his breath under false pretences. And not only must the solution be adequate, but all its data must be given in the body of the story. The author must not suddenly spring a new person or a new circumstance upon his reader at the end. Thus, if a friend were to ask me to guess who dined with him yesterday, it would be fatuous if he had in mind somebody of whom he knew I had never heard. The only person who has ever solved *The Big Bow Mystery* is myself.

This is not paradox but plain fact. For long before the book was written, I said to myself one night that no mystery-monger had ever murdered a man in a room to which there was no possible access. The puzzle was scarcely propounded ere the solution flew up and the idea lay stored in my mind till, years later, during the silly season, the editor of a popular London evening paper, anxious to let the sea-serpent have a year off, asked me to provide him with a more original piece of fiction. I might have refused, but there was murder in my soul, and here was the opportunity. I went to work seriously, though the *Morning Post* subsequently said the skit was too laboured, and I succeeded at least in exciting my readers, so many of whom sent in unsolicited testimonials in the shape of solutions during the run of the story that, when it ended, the editor asked me to say something by way of acknowledgement. Thereupon I wrote a letter to the paper, thanking the would-be solvers for their kindly attempts to help me out of the mess into which I had got the plot. I did not like to wound their feelings by saying straight out that they had failed, one and all, to hit on the real murderer, just like real police, so I tried to break the truth to them in a roundabout, mendacious fashion, as thus:

To the Editor of *The Star*.

Sir: Now that *The Big Bow Mystery* is solved to the satisfaction of at least one person, will you allow that person the use of your invaluable columns to enable him to thank the hundreds of your readers who have favoured him with their kind suggestions and solutions while his tale was running and they were reading? I ask this more especially because great credit is due to them for enabling me to end the story in a manner so satisfactory to myself. When I started it, I had, of course, no idea who had done the murder, but I was determined no one should guess it. Accordingly, as each correspondent sent in the name of a suspect, I determined he or she should not be the guilty party. By degrees every one of the characters got ticked off as innocent—all except one, and I had no option but to make that character the murderer. I was very sorry to do this, as I rather liked that particular person, but when one has such ingenious readers, what can one do? You can't let anybody boast that he guessed aright, and, in spite of the trouble of altering the plot five or six times, I feel that I have chosen the course most consistent with the dignity of my profession. Had I not been impelled by this consideration I should certainly have brought in a verdict against Mrs Drabdump, as recommended by the reader who said that, judging by the illustration in the *Star*, she must be at least seven feet high, and, therefore, could easily have got on the roof and put her (proportionately) long arm down the chimney to effect the cut. I am not responsible for the artist's conception of the character. When I last saw the good lady she was under six feet, but your artist may have had later information. The *Star* is always so frightfully up to date. I ought not to omit the humorous remark of a correspondent, who said: 'Mortlake might have swung in some wild way from one window to another, at any rate in a story.' I hope my fellow-writers thus satirically prodded will not demand his name, as I object to murders, 'at any rate in real life'. Finally, a word with the legions who have taken me to task for allowing Mr Gladstone to write over 170 words on a postcard. It is all owing to you, sir, who announced my story as containing humorous elements. I tried to put in some, and this gentle dig at the grand old correspondent's habits was intended to be one of them. However, if I am to be taken 'at the foot of the letter' (or rather of the postcard), I must say that only today I received a postcard containing about 250 words. But this was not from Mr Gladstone. At any rate, till Mr Gladstone himself repudiates this postcard, I shall consider myself justified in allowing it to stand in the book.

Again thanking your readers for their valuable assistance,
   Yours, etc.

One would have imagined that nobody could take this
seriously, for it is obvious that the mystery-story is just
the one species of story that cannot be told impromptu or
altered at the last moment, seeing that it demands the most
careful piecing together and the most elaborate dovetailing.
Nevertheless, if you cast your joke upon the waters, you shall
find it no joke after many days. This is what I read in the
Lyttelton Times, New Zealand: 'The chain of circumstantial
evidence seems fairly irrefragable. From all accounts, Mr
Zangwill himself was puzzled, after carefully forging every
link, how to break it. The method ultimately adopted I
consider more ingenious than convincing.' After that I made
up my mind never to joke again, but this good intention now
helps to pave the beaten path.

I. ZANGWILL
London, September 1895

CHAPTER I

On a memorable morning of early December London opened its eyes on a frigid grey mist. There are mornings when King Fog masses his molecules of carbon in serried squadrons in the city, while he scatters them tenuously in the suburbs; so that your morning train may bear you from twilight to darkness. But today the enemy's manoeuvring was more monotonous. From Bow even unto Hammersmith there draggled a dull, wretched vapour, like the wraith of an impecunious suicide come into a fortune immediately after the fatal deed. The barometers and thermometers had sympathetically shared its depression, and their spirits (when they had any) were low. The cold cut like a many-bladed knife.

Mrs Drabdump, of 11 Glover Street, Bow, was one of the few persons in London whom fog did not depress. She went about her work quite as cheerlessly as usual. She had been among the earliest to be aware of the enemy's advent, picking out the strands of fog from the coils of darkness the moment she rolled up her bedroom blind and unveiled the sombre picture of the winter morning. She knew that the fog had come to stay for the day at least, and that the gas bill for the quarter was going to beat the record in high-jumping. She also knew that this was because she had allowed her new gentleman lodger, Mr Arthur Constant, to pay a fixed sum of a shilling a week for gas, instead of charging him a proportion of the actual account for the whole house. The meteorologists might have saved the credit of their science if they had reckoned with Mrs Drabdump's next gas bill when they predicted the weather and made 'Snow' the favourite, and said that 'Fog' would be nowhere. Fog was everywhere, yet Mrs Drabdump took no credit to herself for her prescience.

Mrs Drabdump indeed took no credit for anything, paying her way along doggedly, and struggling through life like a wearied swimmer trying to touch the horizon. That things always went as badly as she had foreseen did not exhilarate her in the least.

Mrs Drabdump was a widow. Widows are not born but made, else you might have fancied Mrs Drabdump had always been a widow. Nature had given her that tall, spare form, and that pale, thin-lipped, elongated, hard-eyed visage, and that painfully precise hair, which are always associated with widowhood in low life. It is only in higher circles that women can lose their husbands and yet remain bewitching. The late Mr Drabdump had scratched the base of his thumb with a rusty nail, and Mrs Drabdump's foreboding that he would die of lockjaw had not prevented her wrestling day and night with the shadow of Death, as she had wrestled with it vainly twice before, when Katie died of diphtheria and little Johnny of scarlet fever. Perhaps it is from overwork among the poor that Death has been reduced to a shadow.

Mrs Drabdump was lighting the kitchen fire. She did it very scientifically, as knowing the contrariety of coal and the anxiety of flaming sticks to end in smoke unless rigidly kept up to the mark. Science was a success as usual; and Mrs Drabdump rose from her knees content, like a Parsee priestess who had duly paid her morning devotions to her deity. Then she started violently, and nearly lost her balance. Her eye had caught the hands of the clock on the mantel. They pointed to fifteen minutes to seven. Mrs Drabdump's devotion to the kitchen fire invariably terminated at fifteen minutes past six. What was the matter with the clock?

Mrs Drabdump had an immediate vision of Snoppet, the neighbouring horologist, keeping the clock in hand for weeks and then returning it only superficially repaired and secretly injured more vitally 'for the good of the trade'. The evil vision vanished as quickly as it came, exorcised by the deep boom of St Dunstan's bells chiming the three-quarters. In its place a great horror surged. Instinct had failed; Mrs Drabdump had risen at half-past six instead of six. Now she understood why she had been feeling so dazed and strange and sleepy. She had overslept herself.

Chagrined and puzzled, she hastily set the kettle over the crackling coal, discovering a second later that she had overslept herself because Mr Constant wished to be woke three-quarters of an hour earlier than usual, and to have his breakfast at seven, having to speak at an early meeting of discontented tram-men. She ran at once, candle in hand, to his bedroom. It was upstairs. All 'upstairs' was Arthur Constant's domain, for it consisted of but two mutually independent rooms. Mrs Drabdump knocked viciously at the door of the one he used for a bedroom, crying, 'Seven o'clock, sir. You'll be late, sir. You must get up at once.' The usual slumberous 'All right' was not forthcoming; but, as she herself had varied her morning salute, her ear was less expectant of the echo. She went downstairs, with no foreboding save that the kettle would come off second best in the race between its boiling and her lodger's dressing.

For she knew there was no fear of Arthur Constant's lying deaf to the call of duty—temporarily represented by Mrs Drabdump. He was a light sleeper, and the tram conductors' bells were probably ringing in his ears, summoning him to the meeting. Why Arthur Constant, B.A.—white-handed and white-shirted, and gentleman to the very purse of him—should concern himself with tram-men, when fortune had confined his necessary relations with drivers to cabmen at the least, Mrs Drabdump could not quite make out. He probably aspired to represent Bow in Parliament; but then it would surely have been wiser to lodge with a landlady who possessed a vote by having a husband alive. Nor was there much practical wisdom in his wish to black his own boots (an occupation in which he shone but little), and to live in every way like a Bow working man. Bow working men were not so lavish in their patronage of water, whether existing in drinking glasses, morning tubs, or laundress's establishments. Nor did they eat the delicacies with which Mrs Drabdump supplied him, with the assurance that they were the artisan's appanage. She could not bear to see him eat things unbefitting his station. Arthur Constant opened his mouth and ate what his landlady gave him, not first deliberately shutting his eyes according to the formula, the rather pluming himself on keeping them very wide open. But it is difficult for saints to see through their own halos; and in practice an aureola about the head is often indistinguishable from a mist.

The tea to be scalded in Mr Constant's pot, when that cantankerous kettle should boil, was not the coarse mixture of black and green sacred to herself and Mr Mortlake, of whom the thoughts of breakfast now reminded her. Poor Mr Mortlake, gone off without any to Devonport, somewhere about four in the fog-thickened darkness of a winter night! Well, she hoped his journey would be duly rewarded, that his perks would be heavy, and that he would make as good a thing out of the 'travelling expenses' as rival labour leaders roundly accused him of to other people's faces. She did not grudge him his gains, nor was it her business if, as they alleged, in introducing Mr Constant to her vacant rooms, his idea was not merely to benefit his landlady. He had done her an uncommon good turn, queer as was the lodger thus introduced. His own apostleship to the sons of toil gave Mrs Drabdump no twinges of perplexity. Tom Mortlake had been a compositor; and apostleship was obviously a profession better paid and of a higher social status. Tom Mortlake—the hero of a hundred strikes—set up in print on a poster, was unmistakably superior to Tom Mortlake setting up other men's names at a case. Still, the work was not all beer and skittles, and Mrs Drabdump felt that Tom's latest job was not enviable. She shook his door as she passed it on her way to the kitchen, but there was no response. The street door was only a few feet off down the passage, and a glance at it dispelled the last hope that Tom had abandoned the journey. The door was unbolted and unchained, and the only security was the latchkey lock. Mrs Drabdump felt a whit uneasy, though, to give her her due, she never suffered as much as most housewives do from criminals who never come. Not quite opposite, but still only a few doors off, on the other side of the street, lived the celebrated ex-detective Grodman, and, illogically enough, his presence in the street gave Mrs Drabdump a curious sense of security, as of a believer living under the shadow of the fane. That any human being of ill-odour should consciously come within a mile of the scent of so famous a sleuth-hound seemed to her highly improbable. Grodman had retired (with a competence) and was only a sleeping dog now; still, even criminals would have sense enough to let him lie.

So Mrs Drabdump did not really feel that there had been any danger, especially as a second glance at the street door showed that Mortlake had been thoughtful enough to slip the loop that held back the bolt of the big lock. She allowed herself another throb of sympathy for the labour leader whirling on his dreary way toward Devonport Dockyard. Not that he had told her anything of his journey beyond the town; but she knew Devonport had a Dockyard because Jessie Dymond—Tom's sweetheart—once mentioned that her aunt lived near there, and it lay on the surface that Tom had gone to help the dockers, who were imitating their London brethren. Mrs Drabdump did not need to be told things to be aware of them. She went back to prepare Mr Constant's superfine tea, vaguely wondering why people were so discontented nowadays. But when she brought up the tea and the toast and the eggs to Mr Constant's sitting-room (which adjoined his bedroom, though without communicating with it), Mr Constant was not sitting in it. She lit the gas, and

laid the cloth; then she returned to the landing and beat at
the bedroom door with an imperative palm. Silence alone
answered her. She called him by name and told him the
hour, but hers was the only voice she heard, and it sounded
strangely to her in the shadows of the staircase. Then,
muttering, 'Poor gentleman, he had the toothache last night;
and p'rhaps he's only just got a wink o' sleep. Pity to disturb
him for the sake of them grizzling conductors. I'll let him
sleep his usual time,' she bore the teapot downstairs with a
mournful, almost poetic, consciousness that soft-boiled eggs
(like love) must grow cold.

Half-past seven came—and she knocked again. But
Constant slept on.

His letters, always a strange assortment, arrived at eight,
and a telegram came soon after. Mrs Drabdump rattled his
door, shouted, and at last put the wire under it. Her heart
was beating fast enough now, though there seemed to be a
cold, clammy snake curling round it. She went downstairs
again and turned the handle of Mortlake's room, and went in
without knowing why. The coverlet of the bed showed that
the occupant had only lain down in his clothes, as if fearing
to miss the early train. She had not for a moment expected
to find him in the room; yet somehow the consciousness
that she was alone in the house with the sleeping Constant
seemed to flash for the first time upon her, and the clammy
snake tightened its folds round her heart.

She opened the street door, and her eye wandered nervously up and down. It was half-past eight. The little street
stretched cold and still in the grey mist, blinking bleary eyes
at either end, where the street lamps smouldered on. No one
was visible for the moment, though smoke was rising from
many of the chimneys to greet its sister mist. At the house of
the detective across the way the blinds were still down and
the shutters up. Yet the familiar, prosaic aspect of the street
calmed her. The bleak air set her coughing; she slammed

the door to, and returned to the kitchen to make fresh tea for Constant, who could only be in a deep sleep. But the canister trembled in her grasp. She did not know whether she dropped it or threw it down, but there was nothing in the hand that battered again a moment later at the bedroom door. No sound within answered the clamour without. She rained blow upon blow in a sort of spasm of frenzy, scarce remembering that her object was merely to wake her lodger, and almost staving in the lower panels with her kicks. Then she turned the handle and tried to open the door, but it was locked. The resistance recalled her to herself—she had a moment of shocked decency at the thought that she had been about to enter Constant's bedroom. Then the terror came over her afresh. She felt that she was alone in the house with a corpse. She sank to the floor, cowering; with difficulty stifling a desire to scream. Then she rose with a jerk and raced down the stairs without looking behind her, and threw open the door and ran out into the street, only pulling up with her hand violently agitating Grodman's door-knocker. In a moment the first floor window was raised—the little house was of the same pattern as her own—and Grodman's full fleshy face loomed through the fog in sleepy irritation from under a nightcap. Despite its scowl the ex-detective's face dawned upon her like the sun upon an occupant of the haunted chamber.

'What in the devil's the matter?' he growled. Grodman was not an early bird, now that he had no worms to catch. He could afford to despise proverbs now, for the house in which he lived was his, and he lived in it because several other houses in the street were also his, and it is well for the landlord to be about his own estate in Bow, where poachers often shoot the moon. Perhaps the desire to enjoy his greatness among his early cronies counted for something, too, for he had been born and bred at Bow, receiving when a youth his first engagement from the local police quarters, whence he drew a few shillings a week as an amateur detective in his leisure hours.

Grodman was still a bachelor. In the celestial matrimonial bureau a partner might have been selected for him, but he had never been able to discover her. It was his one failure as a detective. He was a self-sufficing person, who preferred a gas stove to a domestic; but in deference to Glover Street opinion he admitted a female factotum between ten a.m. and ten p.m., and, equally in deference to Glover Street opinion, excluded her between ten p.m. and ten a.m.

'I want you to come across at once,' Mrs Drabdump gasped. 'Something has happened to Mr Constant.'

'What! Not bludgeoned by the police at the meeting this morning, I hope?'

'No, no! He didn't go. He is dead.'

'Dead?' Grodman's face grew very serious now.

'Yes. Murdered!'

'What?' almost shouted the ex-detective. 'How? When? Where? Who?'

'I don't know. I can't get to him. I have beaten at his door. He does not answer.'

Grodman's face lit up with relief.

'You silly woman! Is that all? I shall have a cold in my head. Bitter weather. He's dog-tired after yesterday—processions, three speeches, kindergarten, lecture on "the moon", article on co-operation. That's his style.' It was also Grodman's style. He never wasted words.

'No,' Mrs Drabdump breathed up at him solemnly, 'he's dead.'

'All right; go back. Don't alarm the neighbourhood unnecessarily. Wait for me. Down in five minutes.' Grodman did not take this Cassandra of the kitchen too seriously. Probably he knew his woman. His small, bead-like eyes glittered with an almost amused smile as he withdrew them from Mrs Drabdump's ken, and shut down the sash with a bang. The poor woman ran back across the road and through her door, which she would not close behind her. It seemed to shut her in with the dead. She waited in the passage. After an age—seven minutes by any honest clock—Grodman made his appearance, looking as dressed as usual, but with unkempt hair and with disconsolate side-whisker. He was not quite used to that side-whisker yet, for it had only recently come within the margin of cultivation. In active service Grodman had been clean-shaven, like all members of *the* profession— for surely your detective is the most versatile of actors. Mrs Drabdump closed the street door quietly, and pointed to the stairs, fear operating like a polite desire to give him prece- dence. Grodman ascended, amusement still glimmering in his eyes. Arrived on the landing he knocked peremptorily at the door, crying, 'Nine o'clock, Mr Constant; nine o'clock!' When he ceased there was no other sound or movement. His face grew more serious. He waited, then knocked, and cried louder. He turned the handle, but the door was fast. He tried to peer through the keyhole, but it was blocked. He shook the upper panels, but the door seemed bolted as well as locked. He stood still, his face set and rigid, for he liked and esteemed the man.

'Ay, knock your loudest,' whispered the pale-faced woman. 'You'll not wake him now.'

The grey mist had followed them through the street door, and hovered about the staircase, charging the air with a moist, sepulchral odour.

'Locked and bolted,' muttered Grodman, shaking the door afresh.

'Burst it open,' breathed the woman, trembling violently all over, and holding her hands before her as if to ward off the dreadful vision. Without another word, Grodman applied his shoulder to the door, and made a violent muscular effort. He had been an athlete in his time, and the sap was yet in him. The door creaked, little by little it began to give, the woodwork enclosing the bolt of the lock splintered, the panels bent upward, the large upper bolt tore off its iron staple; the door flew back with a crash. Grodman rushed in.

'My God!' he cried. The woman shrieked. The sight was too terrible.

Within a few hours the jubilant news-boys were shrieking 'Horrible Suicide in Bow,' and *The Moon* poster added, for the satisfaction of those too poor to purchase: 'A Philanthropist Cuts His Throat.'

CHAPTER II

BUT the newspapers were premature. Scotland Yard refused to prejudice the case despite the penny-a-liners. Several arrests were made, so that the later editions were compelled to soften 'Suicide' into 'Mystery'. The people arrested were a nondescript collection of tramps. Most of them had committed other offences for which the police had not arrested them. One bewildered-looking gentleman gave himself up (as if he were a riddle), but the police would have none of him, and restored him forthwith to his friends and keepers. The number of candidates for each new opening in Newgate is astonishing.

The full significance of this tragedy of a noble young life cut short had hardly time to filter into the public mind, when a fresh sensation absorbed it. Tom Mortlake had been arrested the same day at Liverpool on suspicion of being concerned in the death of his fellow-lodger. The news fell like a bombshell upon a land in which Tom Mortlake's name was a household word. That the gifted artisan orator, who had never shrunk upon occasion from launching red rhetoric at Society, should actually have shed blood seemed too startling, especially as the blood shed was not blue, but the property of a lovable young middle-class idealist, who had now literally given his life to the Cause. But this supplementary sensation did not grow to a head, and everybody (save a few labour leaders) was relieved to hear that Tom had been released almost immediately, being merely subpoenaed to appear at the inquest. In an interview which he accorded to the representative of a Liverpool paper the same afternoon, he stated that he put his arrest down entirely to the enmity and rancour entertained towards him by the police throughout the country. He had come to Liverpool to trace the movements of a friend about whom he was very uneasy, and he was making anxious inquiries at the docks to discover at what times steamers left for America, when the detectives stationed there in accordance with instructions from headquarters had arrested him as a suspicious-looking character. 'Though,' said Tom, 'they must very well have known my phiz, as I have been sketched and caricatured all over the shop. When I told them who I was they had the decency to let me go. They thought they'd scored off me enough, I reckon. Yes, it certainly *is* a strange coincidence that I might actually have had something to do with the poor fellow's death, which has cut me up as much as anybody; though if they had known I had just come from the "scene of the crime", and actually lived in the house, they would probably have—let me alone.' He laughed sarcastically. 'They are a queer lot of muddle-heads are the police. Their motto is, "First catch your man, then cook the evidence". If you're on the spot you're guilty because you're there, and if you're elsewhere you're guilty because you have gone away. Oh, I know them! If they could have seen their way to clap me in quod, they'd ha' done it. Lucky I know the number of the cabman who took me to Euston before five this morning.'

'If they clapped you in quod,' the interviewer reported himself as facetiously observing, 'the prisoners would be on strike in a week.'

'Yes, but there would be so many blacklegs ready to take their places,' Mortlake flashed back, 'that I'm afraid it 'ould be no go. But do excuse me. I am so upset about my friend. I'm afraid he has left England, and I have to make inquiries; and now there's poor Constant gone—horrible! horrible! and I'm due in London at the inquest. I must really run away. Goodbye. Tell your readers it's all a police grudge.'

'One last word, Mr Mortlake, if you please. Is it true that you were billed to preside at a great meeting of clerks at St James's Hall between one and two today to protest against the German invasion?'

'Whew! So I was. But the beggars arrested me just before one, when I was going to wire, and then the news of poor Constant's end drove it out of my head. What a nuisance! Lord, how troubles do come together! Well, goodbye, send me a copy of the paper.'

Tom Mortlake's evidence at the inquest added little beyond this to the public knowledge of his movements on the morning of the Mystery. The cabman who drove him to Euston had written indignantly to the papers to say that he had picked up his celebrated fare at Bow Railway Station at about half-past four a.m., and the arrest was a deliberate insult to democracy, and he offered to make an affidavit to that effect, leaving it dubious to which effect. But Scotland Yard betrayed no itch for the affidavit in question, and No. 2138 subsided again into the obscurity of his rank. Mortlake—whose face was very pale below the black mane brushed back from his fine forehead—gave his evidence in low, sympathetic tones. He had known the deceased for over a year, coming constantly across him in their common political and social work, and had found the furnished rooms for him in Glover Street at his own request, they just being to let when Constant resolved to leave his rooms at Oxford House in Bethnal Green and to share the actual life of the people. The locality suited the deceased, as being near the People's Palace. He respected and admired the deceased, whose genuine goodness had won all hearts. The deceased was an untiring worker; never grumbled, was always in fair spirits, regarded his life and wealth as a sacred trust to be used for the benefit of humanity. He had last seen him at a quarter past nine p.m. on the day preceding his death. He (witness) had received a letter by the last post which made him uneasy about a friend. Deceased was evidently suffering from toothache, and was fixing a piece of cotton-wool in a hollow tooth, but he did not complain. Deceased seemed rather upset by the news he brought, and they both discussed it rather excitedly.

By a JURYMAN: Did the news concern him?

MORTLAKE: Only impersonally. He knew my friend, and was keenly sympathetic when one was in trouble.

CORONER: Could you show the jury the letter you received?

MORTLAKE: I have mislaid it, and cannot make out where it has got to. If you, sir, think it relevant or essential, I will state what the trouble was.

CORONER: Was the toothache very violent?

MORTLAKE: I cannot tell. I think not, though he told me it had disturbed his rest the night before.

CORONER: What time did you leave him?

MORTLAKE: About twenty to ten.

CORONER: And what did you do then?

MORTLAKE: I went out for an hour or so to make some inquiries. Then I returned, and told my landlady I should be leaving by an early train for—for the country.

CORONER: And that was the last you saw of the deceased?

MORTLAKE (*with emotion*): The last.

CORONER: How was he when you left him?

MORTLAKE: Mainly concerned about my trouble.

CORONER: Otherwise you saw nothing unusual about him?

MORTLAKE: Nothing.

CORONER: What time did you leave the house on Tuesday morning?

MORTLAKE: At about five and twenty minutes past four.

CORONER: Are you sure that you shut the street door?

MORTLAKE: Quite sure. Knowing my landlady was rather a timid person, I even slipped the bolt of the big lock, which was usually tied back. It was impossible for anyone to get in even with a latchkey.

Mrs Drabdump's evidence (which, of course, preceded his) was more important, and occupied a considerable time, unduly eked out by Drabdumpian padding. Thus she not only deposed that Mr Constant had the toothache, but that it was going to last about a week; in tragi-comic indifference to the radical cure that had been effected. Her account of the last hours of the deceased tallied with Mortlake's, only that she feared Mortlake was quarrelling with him over something in the letter that came by the nine o'clock post. Deceased had left the house a little after Mortlake, but had returned before him, and had gone straight to his bedroom. She had not actually seen him come in, having been in the kitchen, but she heard his latchkey, followed by his light step up the stairs.

A JURYMAN: How do you know it was not somebody else? (*Sensation, of which the juryman tries to look unconscious.*)

WITNESS: He called down to me over the banisters, and says in his sweetish voice: 'Be hextra sure to wake me at a quarter to seven, Mrs Drabdump, or else I shan't get to my tram meeting.'

(*Juryman collapses.*)

CORONER: And did you wake him?

MRS DRABDUMP (*breaking down*): Oh, my lud, how can you ask?

CORONER: There, there, compose yourself. I mean did you try to wake him?

MRS DRABDUMP: I have taken in and done for lodgers this seventeen years, my lud, and have always gave satisfaction; and Mr Mortlake, he wouldn't ha' recommended me otherwise, though I wish to Heaven the poor gentleman had never—

CORONER: Yes, yes, of course. You tried to rouse him?

But it was some time before Mrs Drabdump was sufficiently calm to explain that though she had overslept herself, and though it would have been all the same anyhow, she *had* come up to time. Bit by bit the tragic story was forced from her lips—a tragedy that even her telling could not make tawdry. She told with superfluous detail how—when Mr Grodman broke in the door—she saw her unhappy gentleman lodger lying on his back in bed, stone dead, with a gaping red wound in his throat; how her stronger-minded companion calmed her a little by spreading a handkerchief over the distorted face; how they then looked vainly about and under the bed for any instrument by which the deed could have been done, the veteran detective carefully making a rapid inventory of the contents of the room, and taking notes of the precise position and condition of the body before anything was disturbed by the arrival of gapers or bunglers; how she had pointed out to him that both the windows were firmly bolted to keep out the cold night air; how, having noted this down with a puzzled, pitying shake of the head, he had opened the window to summon the police, and espied in the fog one Denzil Cantercot, whom he called and told to run to the nearest police station and ask them to send on an inspector and a surgeon. How they both remained in the room till the police arrived, Grodman pondering deeply the while and making notes every now and again, as fresh points occurred to him, and asking her questions about the poor, weak-headed young man. Pressed as to what she meant by calling the deceased 'weak-headed', she replied that some of her neighbours wrote him begging letters, though, Heaven knew, they were better off than herself, who had to scrape her fingers to the bone for every penny she earned. Under further pressure from Mr Talbot, who was watching the inquiry on behalf of Arthur Constant's family, Mrs Drabdump admitted that the deceased had behaved like a human being, nor was there anything externally eccentric or queer in his conduct. He was always cheerful and pleasant spoken, though certainly soft—God rest his soul. No; he never shaved, but wore all the hair that Heaven had given him.

By a JURYMAN: She thought deceased was in the habit of locking his door when he went to bed. Of course, she couldn't say for certain. (*Laughter.*) There was no need to bolt the door as well. The bolt slid upward, and was at the top of the door. When she first let lodgings, her reasons for which she seemed anxious to publish, there had only been a bolt, but a suspicious lodger, she would not call him a gentleman, had complained that he could not fasten his door behind him, and so she had been put to the expense of having a lock made. The complaining lodger went off soon after without paying his rent. (*Laughter.*) She had always known he would.

CORONER: Was deceased at all nervous?

WITNESS: No, he was a very nice gentleman. (*A laugh.*)

CORONER: I mean did he seem afraid of being robbed?

WITNESS: No, he was always goin' to demonstrations. (*Laughter.*) I told him to be careful. I told him I lost a purse with 3s. 2d. myself on Jubilee Day.

Mrs Drabdump resumed her seat, weeping vaguely.

CORONER: Gentlemen, we shall have an opportunity of viewing the room shortly.

The story of the discovery of the body was retold, though more scientifically, by MR GEORGE GRODMAN, whose unexpected resurgence into the realm of his early exploits excited as keen a curiosity as the reappearance 'for this occasion only' of a retired prima donna. His book, *Criminals I Have Caught*, passed from the twenty-third to the twenty-fourth edition merely on the strength of it. Mr Grodman stated that the body was still warm when he found it. He thought that death was quite recent. The door he had had to burst was bolted as well as locked. He confirmed Mrs Drabdump's statement about the windows; the chimney was very narrow. The cut looked as if done by a razor. There was no instrument lying about the room. He had known the deceased about a month. He seemed a very earnest, simple-minded young fellow who spoke a great deal about the brotherhood of man. (The hardened old man-hunter's voice was not free from a tremor as he spoke jerkily of the dead man's enthusiasms.) He should have thought the deceased the last man in the world to commit suicide.

MR DENZIL CANTERCOT was next called. He was a poet. (*Laughter.*) He was on his way to Mr Grodman's house to tell him he had been unable to do some writing for him because he was suffering from writer's cramp, when Mr Grodman called to him from the window of No. 11 and asked him to run for the police. No, he did not run; he was a philosopher. (*Laughter.*) He returned with them to the door, but did not go up. He had no stomach for crude sensations. (*Laughter.*) The grey fog was sufficiently unbeautiful for him for one morning. (*Laughter.*)

INSPECTOR HOWLETT said: About 9:45 on the morning of Tuesday, 4th December, from information received, he went with Sergeant Runnymede and Dr Robinson to 11 Glover Street, Bow, and there found the dead body of a young man, lying on his back with his throat cut. The door of the room had been smashed in, and the lock and the bolt evidently forced. The room was tidy. There were no marks of blood on the floor. A purse full of gold was on the dressing-table beside a big book. A hip-bath with cold water stood beside the bed, over which was a hanging bookcase. There was a large wardrobe against the wall next to the door. The chimney was very narrow. There were two windows, one bolted. It was about eighteen feet to the pavement. There was no way of climbing up. No one could possibly have got out of the room, and then bolted the doors and windows behind him; and he had searched all parts of the room in which anyone might have been concealed. He had been unable to find any instrument in the room, in spite of exhaustive search, there being not even a penknife in the pockets of the clothes of the deceased, which lay on a chair. The house and the back yard, and the adjacent pavement, had also been fruitlessly searched.

SERGEANT RUNNYMEDE made an identical statement, saving only that *he* had gone with Dr Robinson and Inspector Howlett.

DR ROBINSON, divisional surgeon, said: The deceased was lying on his back, with his throat cut. The body was not yet cold, the abdominal region being quite warm. Rigor mortis had set in in the lower jaw, neck and upper extremities. The muscles contracted when beaten. I inferred that life had been extinct some two or three hours, probably not longer, it might have been less. The bedclothes would keep the lower part warm for some time. The wound, which was a deep one, was five and a half inches from right to left across the throat to a point under the left ear. The upper portion of the windpipe was severed, and likewise the jugular vein. The muscular coating of the carotid artery was divided. There was a slight cut, as if in continuation of the wound, on the thumb of the left hand. The hands were clasped underneath the head. There was no blood on the right hand. The wound could not have been self-inflicted. A sharp instrument had been used, such as a razor. The cut might have been made by a left-handed person. No doubt death was practically instantaneous. I saw no signs of a struggle about the body or the room. I noticed a purse on the dressing-table, lying next to Madame Blavatsky's big book on Theosophy. Sergeant Runnymede drew my attention to the fact that the door had evidently been locked and bolted from within.

By a JURYMAN: I do not say the cuts could not have been made by a right-handed person. I can offer no suggestion as to how the inflicter of the wound got in or out. Extremely improbable that the cut was self-inflicted. There was little trace of the outside fog in the room.

POLICE-CONSTABLE WILLIAMS said he was on duty in the early hours of the morning of the 4th inst. Glover Street lay within his beat. He saw or heard nothing suspicious. The fog was never very dense, though nasty to the throat. He had passed through Glover Street about half-past four. He had not seen Mr Mortlake or anybody else leave the house.

The Court here adjourned, the Coroner and the jury repairing in a body to 11 Glover Street to view the house and the bedroom of the deceased. And the evening posters announced: 'The Bow Mystery Thickens'.

CHAPTER III

BEFORE the inquiry was resumed, all the poor wretches in custody had been released on suspicion that they were innocent; there was not a single case even for a magistrate. Clues, which at such seasons are gathered by the police like blackberries off the hedges, were scanty and unripe. Inferior specimens were offered them by bushels, but there was not a good one among the lot. The police could not even manufacture a clue.

Arthur Constant's death was already the theme of every hearth, railway carriage and public house. The dead idealist had points of contact with so many spheres. The East End and West End alike were moved and excited, the Democratic Leagues and the Churches, the Doss-houses and the Universities. The pity of it! And then the impenetrable mystery of it!

The evidence given in the concluding portion of the investigation was necessarily less sensational. There were no more witnesses to bring the scent of blood over the coroner's table; those who had yet to be heard were merely relatives and friends of the deceased, who spoke of him as he had been in life. His parents were dead, perhaps luckily for them; his relatives had seen little of him, and had scarce heard as much about him as the outside world. No man is a prophet in his own country, and, even if he migrates, it is advisable for him to leave his family at home. His friends were a motley crew; friends of the same friend are not necessarily friends of one another. But their diversity only made the congruity of the tale they had to tell more striking. It was the tale of a man who had never made an enemy even by benefiting him, nor lost a friend even by refusing his favours; the tale of a man

26

whose heart overflowed with peace and goodwill to all men all the year round; of a man to whom Christmas came not once, but three hundred and sixty-five times a year; it was the tale of a brilliant intellect, who gave up to mankind what was meant for himself, and worked as a labourer in the vineyard of humanity, never crying that the grapes were sour; of a man uniformly cheerful and of good courage, living in that forgetfulness of self which is the truest antidote to despair. And yet there was not quite wanting the note of pain to jar the harmony and make it human. Richard Elton, his chum from boyhood, and vicar of Somerton in Midlandshire, handed to the coroner a letter from the deceased about ten days before his death, containing some passages which the coroner read aloud: 'Do you know anything of Schopenhauer? I mean anything beyond the current misconceptions? I have been making his acquaintance lately. He is an agreeable rattle of a pessimist; his essay on "The Misery of Mankind" is quite lively reading. At first his assimilation of Christianity and Pessimism (it occurs in his essay on "Suicide") dazzled me as an audacious paradox. But there is truth in it. Verily, the whole creation groaneth and travaileth, and man is a degraded monster, and sin is over all. Ah, my friend, I have shed many of my illusions since I came to this seething hive of misery and wrongdoing. What shall one man's life—a million men's lives—avail against the corruption, the vulgarity and the squalor of civilization? Sometimes I feel like a farthing rushlight in the Hall of Eblis. Selfishness is so long and life so short. And the worst of it is that everybody is so beastly contented. The poor no more desire comfort than the rich culture. The woman to whom a penny school fee for her child represents an appreciable slice of her income is satisfied that the rich we shall always have with us.

'The real crusted old Tories are the paupers in the Workhouse. The Radical working men are jealous of their own leaders, and the leaders of one another. Schopenhauer must have organized a labour party in his salad days. And yet one can't help feeling that he committed suicide as a philosopher by not committing it as a man. He claims kinship with Buddha, too; though Esoteric Buddhism at least seems spheres removed from the philosophy of "The Will and the Idea". What a wonderful woman Madame Blavatsky must be. I can't say I follow her, for she is up in the clouds nearly all the time, and I haven't as yet developed an astral body. Shall I send you on her book? It is fascinating. . . I am becoming quite a fluent orator. One soon gets into the way of it. The horrible thing is that you catch yourself saying things to lead up to "Cheers" instead of sticking to the plain realities of the business. Lucy is still doing the galleries in Italy. It used to pain me sometimes to think of my darling's happiness when I came across a flat-chested factory girl. Now I feel her happiness is as important as a factory girl's.'

Lucy, the witness explained, was Lucy Brent, the betrothed of the deceased. The poor girl had been telegraphed for, and had started for England. The witness stated that the outburst of despondency in this letter was almost a solitary one, most of the letters in his possession being bright, buoyant and hopeful. Even this letter ended with a humorous statement of the writer's manifold plans and projects for the New Year. The deceased was a good churchman.

CORONER: Was there any private trouble in his own life to account for the temporary despondency?

WITNESS: Not so far as I am aware. His financial position was exceptionally favourable.

CORONER: There had been no quarrel with Miss Brent?

WITNESS: I have the best authority for saying that no shadow of difference had ever come between them.

CORONER: Was the deceased left-handed?

WITNESS: Certainly not. He was not even ambidextrous.

A JURYMAN: Isn't Shoppinhour one of the infidel writers, published by the Freethought Publication Society?

THE BIG BOW MYSTERY 29

WITNESS: I do not know who publishes his books.

THE JURYMAN (*a small grocer and big raw-boned Scotchman, rejoicing in the name of Sandy Sanderson and the dignities of deaconry and membership of the committee of the Bow Conservative Association*): No equeevocation, sir. Is he not a secularist, who has lectured at the Hall of Science?

WITNESS: No, he is a foreign writer—(*Mr Sanderson was heard to thank Heaven for this small mercy*)—who believes that life is not worth living.

THE JURYMAN: Were you not shocked to find the friend of a meenister reading such impure leeterature?

WITNESS: The deceased read everything. Schopenhauer is the author of a system of philosophy, and not what you seem to imagine. Perhaps you would like to inspect the book? (*Laughter.*)

THE JURYMAN: I would na' touch it with a pitchfork. Such books should be burnt. And this Madame Blavatsky's book— what is that? Is that also pheelosophy?

WITNESS: No. It is Theosophy. (*Laughter.*)

MR ALLEN SMITH, secretary of the Tram-men's Union, stated that he had had an interview with the deceased on the day before his death, when he (the deceased) spoke hopefully of the prospects of the movement, and wrote him out a check for 10 guineas for his union. Deceased promised to speak at a meeting called for a quarter past seven a.m. the next day.

MR EDWARD WIMP, of the Scotland Yard Detective Department, said that the letters and papers of the deceased threw no light upon the manner of his death, and they would be handed back to the family. His Department had not formed any theory on the subject.

The Coroner proceeded to sum up the evidence. 'We have to deal, gentlemen,' he said, 'with a most incomprehensible and mysterious case, the details of which are yet astonishingly simple. On the morning of Tuesday, the 4th inst., Mrs Drabdump, a worthy, hard-working widow, who lets lodgings at 11 Glover Street, Bow, was unable to arouse the deceased, who occupied the entire upper floor of the house. Becoming alarmed, she went across to fetch Mr George Grodman, a gentleman known to us all by reputation, and to whose clear and scientific evidence we are much indebted, and got him to batter in the door. They found the deceased lying back in bed with a deep wound in his throat. Life had only recently become extinct. There was no trace of any instrument by which the cut could have been effected; there was no trace of any person who could have effected the cut. No person could apparently have got in or out. The medical evidence goes to show that the deceased could not have inflicted the wound himself. And yet, gentlemen, there are, in the nature of things, two—and only two—alternative explanations of his death. Either the wound was inflicted by his own hand, or it was inflicted by another's. I shall take each of these possibilities separately. First, did the deceased commit suicide? The medical evidence says deceased was lying with his hands clasped behind his head. Now the wound was made from right to left, and terminated by a cut on the left thumb. If the deceased had made it he would have had to do it with his right hand, while his left hand remained under his head—a most peculiar and unnatural position to assume. Moreover, in making a cut with the right hand, one would naturally move the hand from left to right. It is unlikely that the deceased would move his right hand so awkwardly and unnaturally, unless, of course, his object was to baffle suspicion. Another point is that on this hypothesis, the deceased would have had to replace his right hand beneath his head. But Dr Robinson believes that death was instantaneous. If so, deceased could have had no time to pose so neatly. It is just possible the cut was made with the left hand, but then the deceased was right-handed. The absence of any signs of a possible weapon undoubtedly goes to corroborate the medical evidence. The police have made an exhaustive search in all places where the razor or other weapon or instrument might by any possibility have been concealed, including the bedclothes, the mattress, the pillow, and the street into which it might have been dropped. But all theories involving the wilful concealment of the fatal instrument have to reckon with the fact or probability that death was instantaneous, also with the fact that there was no blood about the floor. Finally, the instrument used was in all likelihood a razor, and the deceased did not shave, and was never known to be in possession of any such instrument. If, then, we were to confine ourselves to the medical and police evidence, there would, I think, be little hesitation in dismissing the idea of suicide. Nevertheless, it is well to forget the physical aspect of the case for a moment and to apply our minds to an unprejudiced inquiry into the mental aspect of it. Was there any reason why the deceased should wish to take his own life? He was young, wealthy and popular, loving and loved; life stretched fair before him. He had no vices. Plain living, high thinking and noble doing were the three guiding stars of his life. If he had had ambition, an illustrious public career was within reach. He was an orator of no mean power, a brilliant and industrious man. His outlook was always on the future—he was always sketching out ways in which he could be useful to his fellow-men. His purse and his time were ever at the command of whosoever could show fair claim upon them. If such a man were likely to end his own life, the science of human nature would be at an end. Still, some of the shadows of the picture have been presented to us. The man had his moments of despondency—as which of us has not? But they seem to have been few and passing. Anyhow, he was cheerful enough on the day before his death. He was suffering, too, from toothache. But it does not seem to have been violent, nor did he complain. Possibly, of course, the pain became very acute in the night. Nor must we forget that he may have overworked himself, and got his nerves into a morbid state.

He worked very hard, never rising later than half-past seven, and doing far more than the professional 'labour leader'. He taught and wrote as well as spoke and organized. But on the other hand all witnesses agree that he was looking forward eagerly to the meeting of tram-men on the morning of the 4th inst. His whole heart was in the movement. Is it likely that this was the night he would choose for quitting the scene of his usefulness? Is it likely that if he had chosen it, he would not have left letters and a statement behind, or made a last will and testament? Mr Wimp has found no possible clue to such conduct in his papers. Or is it likely he would have concealed the instrument? The only positive sign of intention is the bolting of his door in addition to the usual locking of it, but one cannot lay much stress on that. Regarding the mental aspects alone, the balance is largely against suicide; looking at the physical aspects, suicide is well nigh impossible. Putting the two together, the case against suicide is all but mathematically complete. The answer, then, to our first question—did the deceased commit suicide?—is that he did not.'

The coroner paused, and everybody drew a long breath. The lucid exposition had been followed with admiration. If the coroner had stopped now, the jury would have unhesitatingly returned a verdict of 'murder'. But the coroner swallowed a mouthful of water and went on:

'We now come to the second alternative—was the deceased the victim of homicide? In order to answer that question in the affirmative it is essential that we should be able to form some conception of the *modus operandi*. It is all very well for Dr Robinson to say the cut was made by another hand; but in the absence of any theory as to how the cut could possibly have been made by that other hand, we should be driven back to the theory of self-infliction, however improbable it may seem to medical gentlemen. Now, what are the facts? When Mrs Drabdump and Mr Grodman found the

body it was yet warm, and Mr Grodman, a witness fortunately qualified by special experience, states that death had
been quite recent. This tallies closely enough with the view
of Dr Robinson, who, examining the body about an hour
later, put the time of death at two or three hours before, say
seven o'clock. Mrs Drabdump had attempted to wake the
deceased at a quarter to seven, which would put back the act
to a little earlier. As I understand from Dr Robinson, that it
is impossible to fix the time very precisely, death may have
very well taken place several hours before Mrs Drabdump's
first attempt to wake deceased. Of course, it may have taken
place between the first and second calls, as he may merely
have been sound asleep at first; it may also not impossibly
have taken place considerably earlier than the first call, for
all the physical data seem to prove. Nevertheless, on the
whole, I think we shall be least likely to err if we assume the
time of death to be half-past six. Gentlemen, let us picture
to ourselves No. 11 Glover Street at half-past six. We have
seen the house; we know exactly how it is constructed. On
the ground floor a front room tenanted by Mr Mortlake, with
two windows giving on the street, both securely bolted; a
back room occupied by the landlady; and a kitchen. Mrs
Drabdump did not leave her bedroom till half-past six, so
that we may be sure all the various doors and windows
have not yet been unfastened; while the season of the year
is a guarantee that nothing had been left open. The front
door through which Mr Mortlake has gone out before half-
past four, is guarded by the latchkey lock and the big lock.
On the upper floor are two rooms—a front room used by
deceased for a bedroom, and a back room which he used
as a sitting-room. The back room has been left open, with
the key inside, but the window is fastened. The door of the
front room is not only locked, but bolted. We have seen the
splintered mortice and the staple of the upper bolt violently
forced from the woodwork and resting on the pin. The

windows are bolted, the fasteners being firmly fixed in the catches. The chimney is too narrow to admit of the passage of even a child. This room, in fact, is as firmly barred in as if besieged. It has no communication with any other part of the house. It is as absolutely self-centred and isolated as if it were a fort in the sea or a log-hut in the forest. Even if any strange person is in the house, nay, in the very sitting-room of the deceased, he cannot get into the bedroom, for the house is one built for the poor, with no communication between the different rooms, so that separate families, if need be, may inhabit each. Now, however, let us grant that some person has achieved the miracle of getting into the front room, first floor, 18 feet from the ground. At half-past six, or thereabouts, he cuts the throat of the sleeping occupant. How is he then to get out without attracting the attention of the now roused landlady? But let us concede him that miracle, too. How is he to go away and yet leave the doors and windows locked and bolted from within? This is a degree of miracle at which my credulity must draw the line. No, the room had been closed all night—there is scarce a trace of fog in it. No one could get in or out. Finally, murders do not take place without motive. Robbery and revenge are the only conceivable motives. The deceased had not an enemy in the world; his money and valuables were left untouched. Everything was in order. There were no signs of a struggle. The answer then to our second inquiry—was the deceased killed by another person?—is, that he was not.

'Gentlemen, I am aware that this sounds impossible and contradictory. But it is the facts that contradict themselves. It seems clear that the deceased did not commit suicide. It seems equally clear that the deceased was not murdered. There is nothing for it, therefore, gentlemen, but to return a verdict tantamount to an acknowledgment of our incompetence to come to any adequately grounded conviction whatever as to the means or the manner by which the deceased met his death. It is the most inexplicable mystery in all my experience.' (*Sensation.*)

THE FOREMAN (*after a colloquy with Mr Sandy Sanderson*): We are not agreed, sir. One of the jurors insists on a verdict of 'Death from visitation by the act of God'.

CHAPTER IV

But Sandy Sanderson's burning solicitude to fix the crime flickered out in the face of opposition, and in the end he bowed his head to the inevitable 'open verdict'. Then the floodgates of inkland were opened, and the deluge pattered for nine days on the deaf coffin where the poor idealist mouldered. The tongues of the Press were loosened, and the leader writers revelled in recapitulating the circumstances of 'The Big Bow Mystery', though they could contribute nothing but adjectives to the solution. The papers teemed with letters—it was a kind of Indian summer of the silly season. But the editors could not keep them out, nor cared to. The mystery was the one topic of conversation everywhere—it was on the carpet and the bare boards alike, in the kitchen and the drawing-room. It was discussed with science or stupidity, with aspirates or without. It came up for breakfast with the rolls, and was swept off the supper-table with the last crumbs.

No. 11 Glover Street, Bow, remained for days a shrine of pilgrimage. The once sleepy little street buzzed from morning till night. From all parts of the town people came to stare up at the bedroom window and wonder with a foolish look of horror. The pavement was often blocked for hours together, and itinerant vendors of refreshment made it a new market centre, while vocalists hastened thither to sing the delectable ditty of the deed without having any voice in the matter. It was a pity the Government did not erect a toll-gate at either end of the street. But Chancellors of the Exchequer rarely avail themselves of the more obvious expedients for paying off the National Debt.

Finally, familiarity bred contempt, and the wits grew facetious at the expense of the Mystery. Jokes on the subject appeared even in the comic papers.

To the proverb, 'You must not say Boo to a goose', one added, 'or else she will explain you the Mystery'. The name of the gentleman who asked whether the Bow Mystery was not 'arrowing shall not be divulged. There was more point in 'Dagonet's' remark that, if he had been one of the unhappy jurymen, he should have been driven to 'suicide'. A professional paradox-monger pointed triumphantly to the somewhat similar situation in 'The Murder in the Rue Morgue', and said that Nature had been plagiarising again—like the monkey she was—and he recommended Poe's publishers to apply for an injunction. More seriously, Poe's solution was re-suggested by 'Constant Reader' as an original idea. He thought that a small organ-grinder's monkey might have got down the chimney with its master's razor, and, after attempting to shave the occupant of the bed, have returned the way it came. This idea created considerable sensation, but a correspondent with a long train of letters draggling after his name pointed out that a monkey small enough to get down so narrow a flue would not be strong enough to inflict so deep a wound. This was disputed by a third writer, and the contest raged so keenly about the power of monkeys' muscles that it was almost taken for granted that a monkey was the guilty party. The bubble was pricked by the pen of 'Common Sense', who laconically remarked that no traces of soot or blood had been discovered on the floor, or on the nightshirt, or the counterpane. The *Lancet*'s leader on the Mystery was awaited with interest. It said: 'We cannot join in the praises that have been showered upon the coroner's summing up. It shows again the evils resulting from having coroners who are not medical men. He seems to have appreciated but inadequately the significance of the medical evidence. He should certainly have directed the jury to return a verdict of murder on that. What was it to do with him that he could see no way by which the wound could have been inflicted by an outside agency? It was for the police to find how that was done. Enough that it was impossible for the unhappy young man to have inflicted such a wound and then have strength and will power enough to hide the instrument and to remove perfectly every trace of his having left the bed for the purpose.'

It is impossible to enumerate all the theories propounded by the amateur detectives, while Scotland Yard religiously held its tongue. Ultimately the interest on the subject became confined to a few papers which had received the best letters. Those papers that couldn't get interesting letters stopped the correspondence and sneered at the 'sensationalism' of those that could. Among the mass of fantasy there were not a few notable solutions, which failed brilliantly, like rockets posing as fixed stars. One was that in the obscurity of the fog the murderer had ascended to the window of the bedroom by means of a ladder from the pavement. He had then with a diamond cut one of the panes away, and effected an entry through the aperture. On leaving he fixed in the pane of glass again (or another which he had brought with him), and thus the room remained with its bolts and locks untouched. On its being pointed out that the panes were too small, a third correspondent showed that that didn't matter, as it was only necessary to insert the hand and undo the fastening, when the entire window could be opened, the process being reversed by the murderer on leaving. This pretty edifice of glass was smashed by a glazier, who wrote to say that a pane could hardly be fixed in from only one side of a window frame, that it would fall out when touched, and that in any case the wet putty could not have escaped detection. A door panel sliced out and replaced was also put forward, and as many trap-doors and secret passages were ascribed to No. 11 Glover Street as if it were a medieval castle. Another of these clever theories was that the murderer was in the room the whole time the police were there—hidden in the wardrobe. Or he had got behind the door when Grodman broke it open, so that he was not noticed in the excitement of the discovery, and escaped with his weapon at the moment when Grodman and Mrs Drabdump were examining the window fastenings.

Scientific explanations also were to hand to explain how the assassin locked and bolted the door behind him. Powerful magnets outside the door had been used to turn the key and push the bolt within. Murderers armed with magnets loomed on the popular imagination like a new microbe. There was only one defect in this ingenious theory—the thing could not be done. A physiologist recalled the conjurers who swallowed swords—by an anatomical peculiarity of the throat—and said that the deceased might have swallowed the weapon after cutting his own throat. This was too much for the public to swallow. As for the idea that the suicide had been effected with a penknife or its blade, or a bit of steel, which had got buried in the wound, not even the quotation of Shelley's line, *'Makes such a wound, the knife is lost in it'*, could secure it a moment's acceptance. The same reception was accorded to the idea that the cut had been made with a candlestick (or other harmless article) constructed like a sword-stick. Theories of this sort caused a humorist to explain that the deceased had hidden the razor in his hollow tooth! Some kind friend of Messrs Maskelyne and Cook suggested that they were the only persons who could have done the deed, as no one else could get out of a locked cabinet. But perhaps the most brilliant of these flashes of false fire was the facetious, yet probably half-seriously meant, letter that appeared in the *Pell Mell Press* under the heading of

'THE BIG BOW MYSTERY SOLVED

'Sir—You will remember that when the Whitechapel murders were agitating the universe, I suggested that the district coroner was the assassin. My suggestion has been disregarded. The coroner is still at large. So is the Whitechapel murderer. Perhaps this suggestive coincidence will incline the authorities to pay more attention to me this time. The problem seems to be this. The deceased could not have cut his own throat. The deceased could not have had his throat cut for him. As one of the two must have happened, this is obvious nonsense. As this is obvious nonsense I am justified in disbelieving it. As this obvious nonsense was primarily put in circulation by Mrs Drabdump and Mr Grodman, I am justified in disbelieving *them*. In short, sir, what guarantee have we that the whole tale is not a cock-and-bull story, invented by the two persons who first found the body? What proof is there that the deed was not done by these persons themselves, who then went to work to smash the door and break the locks and the bolts, and fasten up all the windows before they called the police in?

'I enclose my card, and am, sir, yours truly
    '*One Who Looks Through His Own Spectacles.*'

'[Our correspondent's theory is not so audaciously original as he seems to imagine. Has he not looked through the spectacles of the people who persistently suggested that the Whitechapel murderer was invariably the policeman who found the body? *Somebody* must find the body, if it is to be found at all.—Ed. *P.M.P.*]'

The editor had reason to be pleased that he inserted this letter, for it drew the following interesting communication from the great detective himself:

'THE BIG BOW MYSTERY SOLVED

'Sir—I do not agree with you that your correspondent's theory lacks originality. On the contrary, I think it is delightfully original. In fact it has given me an idea. What that idea is I do not yet propose to say, but if "One Who Looks Through His Own Spectacles" will favour me with his name and address I shall be happy to inform him a little before the rest of the world whether his germ has borne any fruit. I feel he is a kindred spirit, and take this opportunity of saying publicly that I was extremely disappointed at the unsatisfactory verdict. The thing was a palpable assassination; an open verdict has a tendency to relax the exertions of Scotland Yard. I hope I shall not be accused of immodesty, or of making personal reflections, when I say that the Department has had several notorious failures of late. It is not what it used to be. Crime is becoming impertinent. It no longer knows its place, so to speak. It throws down the gauntlet where once it used to cower in its fastnesses. I repeat, I make these remarks solely in the interest of law and order. I do not for one moment believe that Arthur Constant killed himself, and if Scotland Yard satisfies itself with that explanation, and turns on its other side and goes to sleep again, then, sir, one of the foulest and most horrible crimes of the century will for ever go unpunished. My acquaintance with the unhappy victim was but recent; still, I saw and knew enough of the man to be certain (and I hope I have seen and known enough of other men to judge) that he was a man constitutionally incapable of committing an act of violence, whether against himself or anybody else. He would not hurt a fly, as the saying goes. And a man of that gentle stamp always lacks the active energy to lay hands on himself. He was a man to be esteemed in no common degree, and I feel proud to be able to say that he considered me a friend. I am hardly at the time of life at which a man cares to put on his harness again; but, sir, it is impossible that I should ever know a day's rest till the perpetrator of this foul deed is discovered. I have already put myself in communication with the family of the victim, who, I am pleased to say, have every confidence in me, and look to me to clear the name of their unhappy relative from the semi-imputation of suicide. I shall be pleased if anyone who shares my distrust of the authorities, and who has any clue whatever to this

terrible mystery, or any plausible suggestion to offer, if, in
brief, any "One who looks through his own spectacles" will
communicate with me. If I were asked to indicate the direction in which new clues might be most usefully sought, I
should say, in the first instance, anything is valuable that
helps us to piece together a complete picture of the manifold
activities of the man in the East End. He entered one way
or another into the lives of a good many people; is it true
that he nowhere made enemies? With the best intentions a
man may wound or offend; his interference may be resented;
he may even excite jealousy. A young man like the late Mr
Constant could not have had as much practical sagacity as
he had goodness. Whose corns did he tread on? The more
we know of the last few months of his life the more we shall
know of the manner of his death.

'Thanking you by anticipation for the insertion of this
letter in your valuable columns, I am, sir, yours truly,
    'George Grodman.
  '46 Glover Street, Bow.

'P.S.—Since writing the above lines I have, by the kindness
of Miss Brent, been placed in possession of a most valuable
letter, probably the last letter written by the unhappy
gentleman. It is dated Monday, 3rd December, the very eve
of the murder, and was addressed to her at Florence, and
has now, after some delay, followed her back to London
where the sad news unexpectedly brought her. It is a letter
couched, on the whole, in the most hopeful spirit, and
speaks in detail of his schemes. Of course, there are things
in it not meant for the ears of the public, but there can be
no harm in transcribing an important passage:

'"You seem to have imbibed the idea that the East End is a
kind of Golgotha, and this despite that the books out of which
you probably got it are carefully labelled 'Fiction'. Lamb says

somewhere that we think of the 'Dark Ages' as literally without sunlight, and so I fancy people like you, dear, think of the 'East End' as a mixture of mire, misery and murder. How's that for alliteration? Why, within five minutes' walk of me there are the loveliest houses, with gardens back and front, inhabited by very fine people and furniture. Many of my university friends' mouths would water if they knew the income of some of the shopkeepers in the High Road.

"'The rich people about here may not be so fashionable as those in Kensington and Bayswater, but they are every bit as stupid and materialistic. I don't deny, Lucy, I *do* have my black moments, and I do sometimes pine to get away from all this to the lands of sun and lotus-eating. But, on the whole, I am too busy even to dream of dreaming. My real black moments are when I doubt if I am really doing any good. But yet on the whole my conscience or my self-conceit tells me that I am. If one cannot do much with the mass, there is at least the consolation of doing good to the individual. And, after all, is it not enough to have been an influence for good over one or two human souls? There are quite fine characters hereabout—especially in the women—natures capable not only of self-sacrifice, but of delicacy of sentiment. To have learnt to know of such, to have been of service to one or two of such—is not this ample return? I could not get to St James' Hall to hear your friend's symphony at the Henschel concert. I have been reading Mme Blavatsky's latest book, and getting quite interested in occult philosophy. Unfortunately I have to do all my reading in bed, and I don't find the book as soothing a soporific as most new books. For keeping one awake I find Theosophy as bad as toothache. . .'"

'THE BIG BOW MYSTERY SOLVED

'Sir—I wonder if anyone besides myself has been struck by the incredible bad taste of Mr Grodman's letter in your last issue. That he, a former servant of the Department, should publicly insult and run it down can only be charitably explained by the supposition that his judgment is failing him in his old age. In view of this letter, are the relatives of the deceased justified in entrusting him with any private documents? It is, no doubt, very good of him to undertake to avenge one whom he seems snobbishly anxious to claim as a friend; but, all things considered, should not his letter have been headed "The Big Bow Mystery Shelved"?

'I enclose my card, and am, sir, your obedient servant,
'*Scotland Yard.*'

George Grodman read this letter with annoyance, and, crumpling up the paper, murmured scornfully, 'Edward Wimp!'

CHAPTER V

'YES, but what will become of the Beautiful?' said Denzil Cantercot.

'Hang the Beautiful!' said Peter Crowl, as if he were on the committee of the Academy. 'Give me the True.'

Denzil did nothing of the sort. He didn't happen to have it about him.

Denzil Cantercot stood smoking a cigarette in his landlord's shop, and imparting an air of distinction and an agreeable aroma to the close leathery atmosphere. Crowl cobbled away, talking to his tenant without raising his eyes. He was a small, big-headed, sallow, sad-eyed man, with a greasy apron. Denzil was wearing a heavy overcoat with a fur collar. He was never seen without it in public during the winter. In private he removed it and sat in his shirt sleeves. Crowl was a thinker, or thought he was—which seems to involve original thinking anyway. His hair was thinning rapidly at the top, as if his brain was struggling to get as near as possible to the realities of things. He prided himself on having no fads. Few men are without some foible or hobby; Crowl felt almost lonely at times in his superiority. He was a Vegetarian, a Secularist, a Blue Ribbonite, a Republican, and an Anti-tobacconist. Meat was a fad. Drink was a fad. Religion was a fad. Monarchy was a fad. Tobacco was a fad. 'A plain man like me,' Crowl used to say, 'can live without fads.' 'A plain man' was Crowl's catchword. When of a Sunday morning he stood on Mile-end Waste, which was opposite his shop—and held forth to the crowd on the evils of kings, priests and mutton chops, the 'plain man' turned up at intervals like the 'theme' of a symphonic movement. 'I am only a plain man and I want to know.' It was a phrase that sabred the spider-webs

45

of logical refinement, and held them up scornfully on the point. When Crowl went for a little recreation in Victoria Park on Sunday afternoons, it was with this phrase that he invariably routed the supernaturalists. Crowl knew his Bible better than most ministers, and always carried a minutely-printed copy in his pocket, dogs'-eared to mark contradictions in the text. The second chapter of Jeremiah says one thing; the first chapter of Corinthians says another. Two contradictory statements *may* both be true, but 'I am only a plain man, and I want to know'. Crowl spent a large part of his time in setting 'the word against the word'. Cock-fighting affords its votaries no acuter pleasure than Crowl derived from setting two texts by the ears. Crowl had a metaphysical genius which sent his Sunday morning disciples frantic with admiration, and struck the enemy dumb with dismay. He had discovered, for instance, that the Deity could not *move*, owing to already filling all space. He was also the first to invent, for the confusion of the clerical, the crucial case of a saint dying at the Antipodes contemporaneously with another in London. Both went skyward to Heaven, yet the two travelled in directly opposite directions. In all eternity they would never meet. Which, then, got to Heaven? Or was there no such place? 'I am only a plain man, and I want to know.' Preserve us our open spaces; they exist to testify to the incurable interest of humanity in the Unknown and the Misunderstood. Even 'Arry is capable of five minutes' attention to speculative theology, if 'Arriet isn't in a 'urry.

Peter Crowl was not sorry to have a lodger like Denzil Cantercot, who, though a man of parts and thus worth powder and shot, was so hopelessly wrong on all subjects under the sun. In only one point did Peter Crowl agree with Denzil Cantercot—he admired Denzil Cantercot secretly. When he asked him for the True—which was about twice a day on the average—he didn't really expect to get it from him. He knew that Denzil was a poet.

'The Beautiful,' he went on, 'is a thing that only appeals to men like you. The True is for all men. The majority have the first claim. Till then you poets must stand aside. The True and the Useful—that's what we want. The Good of Society is the only test of things. Everything stands or falls by the Good of Society.'

'The Good of Society!' echoed Denzil, scornfully. 'What's the Good of Society? The Individual is before all. The mass must be sacrificed to the Great Man. Otherwise the Great Man will be sacrificed to the mass. Without great men there would be no art. Without art life would be a blank.'

'Ah, but we should fill it up with bread and butter,' said Peter Crowl.

'Yes, it is bread and butter that kills the Beautiful,' said Denzil Cantercot bitterly. 'Many of us start by following the butterfly through the verdant meadows, but we turn aside—'

'To get the grub,' chuckled Peter, cobbling away.

'Peter, if you make a jest of everything, I'll not waste my time on you.'

Denzil's wild eyes flashed angrily. He shook his long hair. Life was very serious to him. He never wrote comic verse intentionally.

There are three reasons why men of genius have long hair. One is, that they forget it is growing. The second is, that they like it. The third is, that it comes cheaper; they wear it long for the same reason that they wear their hats long.

Owing to this peculiarity of genius, you may get quite a reputation for lack of twopence. The economic reason did not apply to Denzil, who could always get credit with the profession on the strength of his appearance. Therefore, when street arabs vocally commanded him to get his hair cut, they were doing no service to barbers. Why does all the world watch over barbers and conspire to promote their interests? Denzil would have told you it was not to serve the barbers, but to gratify the crowd's instinctive resentment of originality. In his palmy days Denzil had been an editor, but he no more thought of turning his scissors against himself than of swallowing his paste. The efficacy of hair has changed since the days of Samson, otherwise Denzil would have been a Hercules instead of a long, thin, nervous man, looking too brittle and delicate to be used even for a pipe-cleaner. The narrow oval of his face sloped to a pointed, untrimmed beard. His linen was reproachable, his dingy boots were down at heel, and his cocked hat was drab with dust. Such are the effects of a love for the Beautiful.

Peter Crowl was impressed with Denzil's condemnation of flippancy, and he hastened to turn off the joke.

'I'm quite serious,' he said. 'Butterflies are no good to nothing or nobody; caterpillars at least save the birds from starving.'

'Just like your view of things, Peter,' said Denzil. 'Good morning, madam.' This to Mrs Crowl, to whom he removed his hat with elaborate courtesy. Mrs Crowl grunted and looked at her husband with a note of interrogation in each eye. For some seconds Crowl stuck to his last, endeavouring not to see the question. He shifted uneasily on his stool. His wife coughed grimly. He looked up, saw her towering over him, and helplessly shook his head in a horizontal direction. It was wonderful how Mrs Crowl towered over Mr Crowl, even when he stood up in his shoes. She measured half an inch less. It was quite an optical illusion.

'Mr Crowl,' said Mrs Crowl, 'then I'll tell him.'

'No, no, my dear, not yet,' faltered Peter helplessly; 'leave it to me.'

'I've left it to you long enough. You'll never do nothing. If it was a question of provin' to a lot of chuckleheads that Jollygee and Genesis, or some other dead and gone Scripture folk that don't consarn no mortal soul, used to contradict each other, your tongue 'ud run thirteen to the dozen. But when it's a matter of takin' the bread out o' the mouths o' your own children, you ain't got no more to say for yourself than a lamp-post. Here's a man stayin' with you for weeks and weeks—eatin' and drinkin' the flesh off your bones—without payin' a far—'

'Hush, hush, mother; it's all right,' said poor Crowl, red as fire.

Denzil looked at her dreamily. 'Is it possible you are alluding to me, Mrs Crowl?' he said.

'Who then should I be alludin' to, Mr Cantercot? Here's seven weeks come and gone, and not a blessed 'aypenny have I—'

'My dear Mrs Crowl,' said Denzil, removing his cigarette from his mouth with a pained air, 'why reproach *me* for your neglect?'

'*My* neglect! I like that!'

'I don't,' said Denzil, more sharply. 'If you had sent me in the bill you would have had the money long ago. How do you expect me to think of these details?'

'We ain't so grand down here. People pays their way—they don't get no *bills*,' said Mrs Crowl, accentuating the word with infinite scorn.

Peter hammered away at a nail, as though to drown his spouse's voice.

'It's three pounds fourteen and eightpence, if you're so anxious to know,' Mrs Crowl resumed. 'And there ain't a woman in the Mile End Road as 'ud a-done it cheaper, with bread at fourpence threefarden a quartern and landlords clamorin' for rent every Monday morning almost afore the sun's up and folks draggin' and slidderin' on till their shoes is only fit to throw after brides, and Christmas comin' and sevenpence a week for schoolin'!'

Peter winced under the last item. He had felt it coming—like Christmas. His wife and he parted company on the question of Free Education. Peter felt that, having brought nine children into the world, it was only fair he should pay a penny a week for each of those old enough to bear educating.

His better half argued that, having so many children, they ought in reason to be exempted. Only people who had few children could spare the penny. But the one point on which the cobbler-sceptic of the Mile End Road got his way was this of the fees. It was a question of conscience, and Mrs Crowl had never made application for their remission, though she often slapped her children in vexation instead. They were used to slapping, and when nobody else slapped them they slapped one another. They were bright, ill-mannered brats, who pestered their parents and worried their teachers, and were happy as the Road was long.

'Bother the school fees!' Peter retorted, vexed. 'Mr Cantercot's not responsible for your children.'

'I should hope not, indeed, Mr Crowl,' Mrs Crowl said sternly. 'I'm ashamed of you.' And with that she flounced out of the shop into the back parlour.

'It's all right,' Peter called after her soothingly. 'The money'll be all right, mother.'

In lower circles it is customary to call your wife your mother; in somewhat superior circles it is the fashion to speak of her as 'the wife' as you speak of 'the Stock Exchange' or 'the Thames', without claiming any peculiar property. Instinctively men are ashamed of being moral and domesticated.

Denzil puffed his cigarette, unembarrassed. Peter bent attentively over his work, making nervous stabs with his awl. There was a long silence. An organ-grinder played a waltz outside, unregarded; and, failing to annoy anybody, moved on. Denzil lit another cigarette. The dirty-faced clock on the shop wall chimed twelve.

'What do you think,' said Crowl, 'of Republics?'

'They are low,' Denzil replied. 'Without a Monarch there is no visible incarnation of Authority.'

'What! do you call Queen Victoria visible?'

'Peter, do you want to drive me from the house? Leave frivolousness to women, whose minds are only large enough for domestic difficulties. Republics are low. Plato mercifully kept the poets out of his. Republics are not congenial soil for poetry.'

'What nonsense! If England dropped its fad of Monarchy and became a Republic tomorrow, do you mean to say that—?'

'I mean to say that there would be no Poet Laureate to begin with.'

'Who's fribbling now, you or me, Cantercot? But I don't care a button-hook about poets, present company always excepted. I'm only a plain man, and I want to know where's the sense of givin' any one person authority over everybody else?'

'Ah, that's what Tom Mortlake used to say. Wait till you're in power, Peter, with trade-union money to control, and working men bursting to give you flying angels and to carry you aloft, like a banner, huzzahing.'

'Ah, that's because he's head and shoulders above 'em already,' said Crowl, with a flash in his sad grey eyes. 'Still, it don't prove that I'd talk any different. And I think you're quite wrong about his being spoiled. Tom's a fine fellow—a man every inch of him, and that's a good many. I don't deny he has his weaknesses, and there was a time when he stood in this very shop and denounced that poor dead Constant. 'Crowl,' said he, 'that man'll do mischief. I don't like these kid-glove philanthropists mixing themselves up in practical labour disputes they don't understand.''

Denzil whistled involuntarily. It was a piece of news.

'I dare say,' continued Crowl, 'he's a bit jealous of anybody's interference with his influence. But in this case the jealousy did wear off, you see, for the poor fellow and he got quite pals, as everybody knows. Tom's not the man to hug a prejudice. However, all that don't prove nothing against Republics. Look at the Czar and the Jews. I'm only a plain man, but I wouldn't live in Russia not for—not for all the leather in it! An Englishman, taxed as he is to keep up his Fad of Monarchy, is at least king in his own castle, whoever bosses it at Windsor. Excuse me a minute, the missus is callin'.'

'Excuse *me* a minute. I'm going, and I want to say before I go—I feel it is only right you should know at once—that after what has passed today I can never be on the same footing here as in the—shall I say pleasant?—days of yore.'

'Oh, no, Cantercot. Don't say that; don't say that!' pleaded the little cobbler.

'Well, shall I say unpleasant, then?'

'No, no, Cantercot. Don't misunderstand me. Mother has been very much put to it lately to rub along. You see she has such a growing family. It grows—daily. But never mind her. You pay whenever you've got the money.'

Denzil shook his head. 'It cannot be. You know when I came here first I rented your top room and boarded myself. Then I learnt to know you. We talked together. Of the Beautiful. And the Useful. I found you had no soul. But you were honest, and I liked you. I went so far as to take my meals with your family. I made myself at home in your back parlour. But the vase has been shattered (I do not refer to that on the mantelpiece), and though the scent of the roses may cling to it still, it can be pieced together—nevermore.' He shook his hair sadly and shambled out of the shop. Crowl would have gone after him, but Mrs Crowl was still calling, and ladies must have the precedence in all polite societies.

Cantercot went straight—or as straight as his loose gait permitted—to 46 Glover Street, and knocked at the door. Grodman's factotum opened it. She was a pock-marked person, with a brickdust complexion and a coquettish manner.

'Oh, here we are again!' she said vivaciously.

'Don't talk like a clown,' Cantercot snapped. 'Is Mr Grodman in?'

'No, you've put him out,' growled the gentleman himself, suddenly appearing in his slippers. 'Come in. What the devil have you been doing with yourself since the inquest? Drinking again?'

'I've sworn off. Haven't touched a drop since—'

'The murder?'

'Eh?' said Denzil Cantercot, startled. 'What do you mean?'

'What I say. Since December 4. I reckon everything from that murder, now, as they reckon longitude from Greenwich.'

'Oh,' said Denzil Cantercot.

'Let me see. Nearly a fortnight. What a long time to keep away from Drink—and Me.'

'I don't know which is worse,' said Denzil, irritated. 'You both steal away my brains.'

'Indeed?' said Grodman, with an amused smile. 'Well, it's only petty pilfering, after all. What's put salt on your wounds?'

'The twenty-fourth edition of my book.'

'*Whose* book?'

'Well, *your* book. You must be making piles of money out of *Criminals I Have Caught.*'

'"Criminals *I* Have Caught",' corrected Grodman. 'My dear Denzil, how often am I to point out that *I* went through the experiences that make the backbone of my book, not *you?* In each case *I* cooked the criminal's goose. Any journalist could have supplied the dressing.'

'The contrary. The journeymen of journalism would have left the truth naked. You yourself could have done that—for there is no man to beat you at cold, lucid, scientific state-ment. But I idealized the bare facts and lifted them into the realm of poetry and literature. The twenty-fourth edition of the book attests my success.'

'Rot! The twenty-fourth edition was all owing to the murder! Did you do that?'

'You take one up so sharply, Mr Grodman,' said Denzil, changing his tone.

'No—I've retired,' laughed Grodman.

Denzil did not reprove the ex-detective's flippancy. He even laughed a little.

'Well, give me another fiver, and I'll cry "quits". I'm in debt.'

'Not a penny. Why haven't you been to see me since the murder? I had to write that letter to the *Pell Mell Press* myself. You might have earned a crown.'

'I've had writer's cramp, and couldn't do your last job. I was coming to tell you so on the morning of the—'

'Murder. So you said at the inquest.'

'It's true.'

'Of course. Weren't you on your oath? It was very zealous of you to get up so early to tell me. In which hand did you have this cramp?'

'Why, in the right, of course.'

'And you couldn't write with your left?'

'I don't think I could even hold a pen.'

'Or any other instrument, mayhap. What had you been doing to bring it on?'

'Writing too much. That is the only possible cause.'

'Oh, I don't know. Writing what?'

Denzil hesitated. 'An epic poem.'

'No wonder you're in debt. Will a sovereign get you out of it?'

'No; it wouldn't be the least use to me.'

'Here it is, then.'

Denzil took the coin and his hat.

'Aren't you going to earn it, you beggar? Sit down and write something for me.'

Denzil got pen and paper, and took his place.

'What do you want me to write?'

'Your Epic Poem.'

Denzil started and flushed. But he set to work. Grodman leaned back in his armchair and laughed, studying the poet's grave face.

Denzil wrote three lines and paused.

'Can't remember any more? Well, read me the start.'

Denzil read:

'Of man's first disobedience and the fruit

Of that forbidden tree whose mortal taste
Brought death into the world—'

'Hold on!' cried Grodman; 'what morbid subjects you choose, to be sure.'

'Morbid! Why, Milton chose the same subject!'

'Blow Milton. Take yourself off—you and your Epics.'

Denzil went. The pock-marked person opened the street door for him.

'When am I to have that new dress, dear?' she whispered coquettishly.

'I have no money, Jane,' he said shortly.

'You have a sovereign.'

Denzil gave her the sovereign, and slammed the door viciously. Grodman overheard their whispers, and laughed silently. His hearing was acute. Jane had first introduced Denzil to his acquaintance about two years ago, when he spoke of getting an amanuensis, and the poet had been doing odd jobs for him ever since. Grodman argued that Jane had her reasons. Without knowing them he got a hold over both. There was no one, he felt, he could not get a hold over. All men—and women—have something to conceal, and you have only to pretend to know what it is. Thus Grodman, who was nothing if not scientific.

Denzil Cantercot shambled home thoughtfully, and abstractedly took his place at the Crowl dinner-table.

CHAPTER VI

MRS CROWL surveyed Denzil Cantercot so stonily and cut him his beef so savagely that he said grace when the dinner was over. Peter fed his metaphysical genius on tomatoes. He was tolerant enough to allow his family to follow their Fads; but no savoury smells ever tempted him to be false to his vegetable loves. Besides, meat might have reminded him too much of his work. There is nothing like leather, but Bow beefsteaks occasionally come very near it.

After dinner Denzil usually indulged in poetic reverie. But today he did not take his nap. He went out at once to 'raise the wind'. But there was a dead calm everywhere. In vain he asked for an advance at the office of the *Mile End Mirror*, to which he contributed scathing leaderettes about vestrymen. In vain he trudged to the city and offered to write the *Ham and Eggs Gazette* an essay on the modern methods of bacon-curing. Denzil knew a great deal about the breeding and slaughtering of pigs, smoke-lofts and drying processes, having for years dictated the policy of the *New Pork Herald* in these momentous matters. Denzil also knew a great deal about many other esoteric matters, including weaving machines, the manufacture of cabbage leaves and snuff, and the inner economy of drain-pipes. He had written for the trade papers since boyhood. But there is great competition on these papers. So many men of literary gifts know all about the intricate technicalities of manufactures and markets, and are eager to set the trade right. Grodman perhaps hardly allowed sufficiently for the step backward that Denzil made when he devoted his whole time for months to *Criminals I Have Caught*. It was as damaging as a debauch. For when your rivals are pushing forward, to stand still is to go back.

In despair Denzil shambled toilsomely to Bethnal Green. He paused before the window of a little tobacconist's shop, wherein was displayed a placard announcing

'Plots For Sale'

The announcement went on to state that a large stock of plots was to be obtained on the premises—embracing sensational plots, humorous plots, love plots, religious plots, and poetic plots; also complete manuscripts, original novels, poems and tales. Apply within.

It was a very dirty-looking shop, with begrimed bricks and blackened woodwork. The window contained some musty old books, an assortment of pipes and tobacco, and a large number of the vilest daubs unhung, painted in oil on Academy boards, and unframed. These were intended for landscapes, as you could tell from the titles. The most expensive was 'Chingford Church', and it was marked 1s. 9d. The others ran from 6d. to 1s. 3d., and were mostly representations of Scottish scenery—a loch with mountains in the background, with solid reflections in the water and a tree in the foreground. Sometimes the tree would be in the background. Then the loch would be in the foreground. Sky and water were intensely blue in all. The name of the collection was 'Original oil paintings done by hand'. Dust lay thick upon everything, as if carefully shovelled on; and the proprietor looked as if he slept in his shop window at night without taking his clothes off. He was a gaunt man with a red nose, long but scanty black locks covered by a smoking cap, and a luxuriant black moustache. He smoked a long clay pipe, and had the air of a broken-down operatic villain.

'Ah, good afternoon, Mr Cantercot,' he said, rubbing his hands, half from cold, half from usage; 'what have you brought me?'

'Nothing,' said Denzil, 'but if you will lend me a sovereign I'll do you a stunner.'

The operatic villain shook his locks, his eyes full of pawky cunning. 'If you did it after that, it *would* be a stunner.'

What the operatic villain did with these plots, and who bought them, Cantercot never knew nor cared to know. Brains are cheap today, and Denzil was glad enough to find a customer.

'Surely you've known me long enough to trust me,' he cried.

'Trust is dead,' said the operatic villain, puffing away.

'So is Queen Anne,' cried the irritated poet. His eyes took a dangerous hunted look. Money he must have. But the operatic villain was inflexible. No plot, no supper.

Poor Denzil went out flaming. He knew not where to turn. Temporarily he turned on his heel again and stared despairingly at the shop window. Again he read the legend:

'PLOTS FOR SALE'

He stared so long at this that it lost its meaning. When the sense of the words suddenly flashed upon him again, they bore a new significance. He went in meekly, and borrowed fourpence off the operatic villain. Then he took the 'bus for Scotland Yard. There was a not ill-looking servant girl in the 'bus. The rhythm of the vehicle shaped itself into rhymes in his brain. He forgot all about his situation and his object. He had never really written an epic—except 'Paradise Lost'—but he composed lyrics about wine and women and often wept to think how miserable he was. But nobody ever bought anything of his, except articles on bacon-curing or attacks on vestrymen. He was a strange, wild creature, and the wench felt quite pretty under his ardent gaze. It almost hypnotized her, though, and she looked down at her new French kid boots to escape it.

At Scotland Yard Denzil asked for Edward Wimp. Edward Wimp was not on view. Like kings and editors, detectives are difficult of approach—unless you are a criminal, when you cannot see anything of them at all. Denzil knew of Edward Wimp, principally because of Grodman's contempt for his successor. Wimp was a man of taste and culture. Grodman's interests were entirely concentrated on the problems of logic and evidence. Books about these formed his sole reading; for *belles lettres* he cared not a straw. Wimp, with his flexible intellect, had a great contempt for Grodman and his slow, laborious, ponderous, almost Teutonic methods. Worse, he almost threatened to eclipse the radiant tradition of Grodman by some wonderfully ingenious bits of workmanship. Wimp was at his greatest in collecting circumstantial evidence; in putting two and two together to make five. He would collect together a number of dark and disconnected data and flash across them the electric light of some unifying hypothesis in a way which would have done credit to a Darwin or a Faraday. An intellect which might have served to unveil the secret workings of nature was subverted to the protection of a capitalistic civilisation.

By the assistance of a friendly policeman, whom the poet magnetized into the belief that his business was a matter of life and death, Denzil obtained the great detective's private address. It was near King's Cross. By a miracle Wimp was at home in the afternoon. He was writing when Denzil was ushered up three pairs of stairs into his presence, but he got up and flashed the bull's-eye of his glance upon the visitor.

'Mr Denzil Cantercot, I believe,' said Wimp.

Denzil started. He had not sent up his name, merely describing himself as a gentleman.

'That is my name,' he murmured.

'You were one of the witnesses at the inquest on the body of the late Arthur Constant. I have your evidence there.' He pointed to a file. 'Why have you come to give fresh evidence?'

Again Denzil started, flushing in addition this time. 'I want money,' he said, almost involuntarily.

'Sit down.' Denzil sat. Wimp stood.

Wimp was young and fresh-coloured. He had a Roman nose, and was smartly dressed. He had beaten Grodman by discovering the wife Heaven meant for him. He had a bouncing boy, who stole jam out of the pantry without anyone being the wiser. Wimp did what work he could do at home in a secluded study at the top of the house. Outside his chamber of horrors he was the ordinary husband of commerce. He adored his wife, who thought poorly of his intellect, but highly of his heart. In domestic difficulties Wimp was helpless. He could not even tell whether the servant's 'character' was forged or genuine. Probably he could not level himself to such petty problems. He was like the senior wrangler who has forgotten how to do quadratics, and has to solve equations of the second degree by the calculus.

'How much money do you want?' he asked.

'I do not make bargains,' Denzil replied, his calm come back by this time. 'I came to tender you a suggestion. It struck me that you might offer me a fiver for my trouble. Should you do so, I shall not refuse it.'

'You shall not refuse it—if you deserve it.'

'Good. I will come to the point at once. My suggestion concerns—Tom Mortlake.'

Denzil threw out the name as if it were a torpedo. Wimp did not move.

'Tom Mortlake,' went on Denzil, looking disappointed, 'had a sweetheart.' He paused impressively.

Wimp said, 'Yes?'

'Where is that sweetheart now?'

'Where, indeed?'

'You know about her disappearance?'

'You have just informed me of it.'

'Yes, she is gone—without a trace. She went about a fortnight before Mr Constant's murder.'

'Murder? How do you know it was a murder?'

'Mr Grodman says so,' said Denzil, startled again.

'H'm! Isn't that rather a proof that it was suicide? Well, go on.'

'About a fortnight before the suicide, Jessie Dymond disappeared. So they tell me in Stepney Green, where she lodged and worked.'

'What was she?'

'She was a dressmaker. She had a wonderful talent. Quite fashionable ladies got to know of it. One of her dresses was presented at Court. I think the lady forgot to pay for it; so Jessie's landlady said.'

'Did she live alone?'

'She had no parents, but the house was respectable.'

'Good-looking, I suppose?'

'As a poet's dream.'

'As yours, for instance?'

'I am a poet; I dream.'

'You dream you are a poet. Well, well! She was engaged to Mortlake?'

'Oh, yes! They made no secret of it. The engagement was an old one. When he was earning 36s. a week as a compositor they were saving up to buy a home. He worked at Railton and Hockes', who print the *New Pork Herald*. I used to take my "copy" into the comps' room, and one day the Father of the Chapel told me all about "Mortlake and his young woman". Ye gods! How times are changed! Two years ago Mortlake had to struggle with my calligraphy—now he is in with all the nobs, and goes to the "At Homes" of the aristocracy.'

'Radical M.P.s,' murmured Wimp, smiling.

'While I am still barred from the dazzling drawing-rooms, where beauty and intellect foregather. A mere artisan! A manual labourer!' Denzil's eyes flashed angrily. He rose with excitement. 'They say he always *was* a jabberer in the composing-room, and he has jabbered himself right out of it and into a pretty good thing. He didn't have much to say about the crimes of capital when he was set up to second the toast of "Railton and Hockes" at the beanfeast.'

'Toast and butter, toast and butter,' said Wimp genially. 'I shouldn't blame a man for serving the two together, Mr Cantercot.'

Denzil forced a laugh. 'Yes; but consistency's *my* motto. I like to see the royal soul immaculate, unchanging, immovable by fortune. Anyhow, when better times came for Mortlake the engagement still dragged on. He did not visit her so much. This last autumn he saw very little of her.'

'How do you know?'

'I—I was often in Stepney Green. My business took me past the house of an evening. Sometimes there was no light in her room. That meant she was downstairs gossiping with the landlady.'

'She might have been out with Tom?'

'No, sir; I knew Tom was on the platform somewhere or other. He was working up to all hours organizing the eight hours working movement.'

'A very good reason for relaxing his sweethearting.'

'It was. He never went to Stepney Green on a week night.'

'But you always did.'

'No—not every night.'

'You didn't go in?'

'Never. She wouldn't permit my visits. She was a girl of strong character. She always reminded me of Flora Macdonald.'

'Another lady of your acquaintance?'

'A lady I know better than the shadows who surround me; who is more real to me than the women who pester me for the price for apartments. Jessie Dymond, too, was of the race of heroines. Her eyes were clear blue, two wells with Truth at the bottom of each. When I looked into those eyes my own were dazzled. They were the only eyes I could never make dreamy.' He waved his hand as if making a pass with it. 'It was she who had the influence over me.'

'You knew her then?'

'Oh, yes. I knew Tom from the old *New Pork Herald* days, and when I first met him with Jessie hanging on his arm he was quite proud to introduce her to a poet. When he got on he tried to shake me off.'

'You should have repaid him what you borrowed.'

'It—it—was only a trifle,' stammered Denzil.

'Yes, but the world turns on trifles,' said the wise Wimp.

'The world is itself a trifle,' said the pensive poet. 'The Beautiful alone is deserving of our regard.'

'And when the Beautiful was not gossiping with her land-lady, did she gossip with you as you passed the door?'

'Alas, no! She sat in her room reading, and cast a shadow—'

'On your life?'

'No; on the blind.'

'Always one shadow?'

'No, sir. Once or twice, two.'

'Ah, you had been drinking.'

'On my life, not. I have sworn off the treacherous wine-cup.'

'That's right. Beer is bad for poets. It makes their feet shaky. Whose was the second shadow?'

'A man's.'

'Naturally. Mortlake's, perhaps?'

'Impossible. He was still striking eight hours.'

'You found out whose? You didn't leave it a shadow of doubt?'

'No; I waited till the substance came out.'

'It was Arthur Constant.'

'You are a magician! You—you terrify me. Yes, it was he.'

'Only once or twice, you say?'

'I didn't keep watch over them.'

'No, no, of course not. You only passed casually. I under-stand you thoroughly.'

Denzil did not feel comfortable at the assertion.

'What did he go there for?' Wimp went on.

'I don't know. I'd stake my soul on Jessie's honour.'

'You might double your stake without risk.'

'Yes, I might! I would! You see her with my eyes.'

'For the moment they are the only ones available. When was the last time you saw the two together?'

'About the middle of November.'

'Mortlake knew nothing of their meetings?'

'I don't know. Perhaps he did. Mr Constant had probably enlisted her in his social mission work. I knew she was one of the attendants at the big children's tea in the Great Assembly Hall early in November. He treated her quite like a lady. She was the only attendant who worked with her hands.'

'The others carried the cups on their feet, I suppose?'

'No; how could that be? My meaning is that all the other attendants were real ladies, and Jessie was only an amateur, so to speak. There was no novelty for her in handing kids cups of tea. I daresay she had helped her landlady often enough at that—there's quite a bushel of brats below stairs. It's almost as bad as at friend Crowl's. Jessie was a real brick. But perhaps Tom didn't know her value. Perhaps he didn't like Constant to call on her, and it led to a quarrel. Anyhow, she's disappeared, like the snowfall on the river. There's not a trace. The landlady, who was such a friend of hers that Jessie used to make up her stuff into dresses for nothing, tells me that she's dreadfully annoyed at not having been left the slightest clue to her late tenant's whereabouts.'

'You have been making inquiries on your own account apparently.'

'Only of the landlady. Jessie never even gave her the week's notice, but paid her in lieu of it, and left immediately. The landlady told me I could have knocked her down with a feather. Unfortunately, I wasn't there to do it, for I should certainly have knocked her down for not keeping her eyes open better. She says if she had only had the least suspicion beforehand that the minx (she dared to call Jessie a minx) was going, she'd have known where, or her name would have been somebody else's. And yet she admits that Jessie was looking ill and worried. Stupid old hag!'

'A woman of character,' murmured the detective.

'Didn't I tell you so?' cried Denzil eagerly. 'Another girl would have let out that she was going. But, no, not a word. She plumped down the money and walked out. The landlady ran upstairs. None of Jessie's things were there. She must have quietly sold them off, or transferred them to the new place. I never in my life met a girl who so thoroughly knew her own mind or had a mind so worth knowing. She always reminded me of the Maid of Saragossa.'

'Indeed! And when did she leave?'

'On the 19th of November.'

'Mortlake of course knows where she is?'

'I can't say. Last time I was at the house to inquire—it was at the end of November—he hadn't been seen there for six weeks. He wrote to her, of course, sometimes—the landlady knew his writing.'

Wimp looked Denzil straight in the eyes, and said, 'You mean, of course, to accuse Mortlake of the murder of Mr Constant?'

'N-n-no, not at all,' stammered Denzil, 'only you know what Mr Grodman wrote to the *Pell Mell*. The more we know about Mr Constant's life the more we shall know about the manner of his death. I thought my information would be valuable to you, and I brought it.'

'And why didn't you take it to Mr Grodman?'

'Because I thought it wouldn't be valuable to *me*.'

'You wrote *Criminals I Have Caught*.'

'How—how do you know that?' Wimp was startling him today with a vengeance.

'Your style, my dear Mr Cantercot. The unique noble style.'

'Yes, I was afraid it would betray me,' said Denzil. 'And since you know, I may tell you that Grodman's a mean curmudgeon. What does he want with all that money and those houses— a man with no sense of the Beautiful? He'd have taken my information, and given me more kicks than ha'pence for it, so to speak.'

'Yes, he is a shrewd man after all. I don't see anything valuable in your evidence against Mortlake.'

'No!' said Denzil in a disappointed tone, and fearing he was going to be robbed. 'Not when Mortlake was already jealous of Mr Constant, who was a sort of rival organizer, unpaid! A kind of blackleg doing the work cheaper—nay, for nothing.'

'Did Mortlake tell you he was jealous?' said Wimp, a shade of sarcastic contempt piercing through his tones.

'Oh, yes! He said to me, "That man will work mischief. I don't like your kid-glove philanthropists meddling in matters they don't understand."'

'Those were his very words?'

'His *ipsissima verba*.'

'Very well. I have your address in my files. Here is a sovereign for you.'

'Only one sovereign! It's not the least use to me.'

'Very well. It's of great use to me. I have a wife to keep.'

'I haven't,' said Denzil with a sickly smile, 'so perhaps I can manage on it after all.' He took his hat and the sovereign.

Outside the door he met a rather pretty servant just bringing in some tea to her master. He nearly upset her tray at sight of her. She seemed more amused at the *rencontre* than he.

'Good afternoon, dear,' she said coquettishly. 'You might let me have that sovereign. I do so want a new Sunday bonnet.'

Denzil gave her the sovereign, and slammed the hall door viciously when he got to the bottom of the stairs. He seemed to be walking arm-in-arm with the long arm of coincidence. Wimp did not hear the duologue. He was already busy on his evening's report to headquarters. The next day Denzil had a body-guard wherever he went. It might have gratified his vanity had he known it. But tonight he was yet unattended, so no one noted that he went to 46 Glover Street, after the early Crowl supper. He could not help going. He wanted to get another sovereign. He also itched to taunt Grodman. Not succeeding in the former object, he felt the road open for the second.

'Do you still hope to discover the Bow murderer?' he asked the old bloodhound.

'I can lay my hand on him now,' Grodman announced curtly.

Denzil hitched his chair back involuntarily. He found conversation with detectives as lively as playing at skittles with bombshells. They got on his nerves terribly, these undemonstrative gentlemen with no sense of the Beautiful.

'But why don't you give him up to justice?' he murmured.

'Ah—it has to be proved yet. But it is only a matter of time.'

'Oh!' said Denzil, 'and shall I write the story for you?'

'No. You will not live long enough.'

Denzil turned white. 'Nonsense! I am years younger than you,' he gasped.

'Yes,' said Grodman, 'but you drink so much.'

CHAPTER VII

WHEN Wimp invited Grodman to eat his Christmas plum-pudding at King's Cross Grodman was only a little surprised. The two men were always overwhelmingly cordial when they met, in order to disguise their mutual detestation. When people really like each other, they make no concealment of their mutual contempt. In his letter to Grodman, Wimp said that he thought it would be nicer for him to keep Christmas in company than in solitary state. There seems to be a general prejudice in favour of Christmas numbers, and Grodman yielded to it. Besides, he thought that a peep at the Wimp domestic interior would be as good as a pantomime. He quite enjoyed the fun that was coming, for he knew that Wimp had not invited him out of mere 'peace and goodwill'.

There was only one other guest at the festive board. This was Wimp's wife's mother's mother, a lady of sweet seventy. Only a minority of mankind can obtain a grandmother-in-law by marrying, but Wimp was not unduly conceited. The old lady suffered from delusions. One of them was that she was a centenarian. She dressed for the part. It is extraordinary what pains ladies will take to conceal their age. Another of Wimp's grandmother-in-law's delusions was that Wimp had married to get her into the family. Not to frustrate his design, she always gave him her company on high-days and holidays. Wilfred Wimp—the little boy who stole the jam—was in great form at the Christmas dinner. The only drawback to his enjoyment was that its sweets needed no stealing. His mother presided over the platters, and thought how much cleverer Grodman was than her husband. When the pretty servant who waited on them was momentarily out of the room, Grodman had remarked that she seemed very inquisitive.

This coincided with Mrs Wimp's own convictions, though Mr Wimp could never be brought to see anything unsatisfactory or suspicious about the girl, not even though there were faults in spelling in the 'character' with which her last mistress had supplied her.

It was true that the puss had pricked up her ears when Denzil Cantercot's name was mentioned. Grodman saw it and watched her, and fooled Wimp to the top of his bent. It was, of course, Wimp who introduced the poet's name, and he did it so casually that Grodman perceived at once that he wished to pump him. The idea that the rival bloodhound should come to him for confirmation of suspicions against his own pet jackal was too funny. It was almost as funny to Grodman that evidence of some sort should be obviously lying to hand in the bosom of Wimp's hand-maiden; so obviously that Wimp could not see it. Grodman enjoyed his Christmas dinner, secure that he had not found a successor after all. Wimp, for his part, contemptuously wondered at the way Grodman's thought hovered about Denzil without grazing the truth. A man constantly about him, too!

'Denzil is a man of genius,' said Grodman. 'And as such comes under the heading of Suspicious Characters. He has written an Epic Poem and read it to me. It is morbid from start to finish. There is "death" in the third line. I daresay you know he polished up my book.' Grodman's artlessness was perfect.

'No. You surprise me,' Wimp replied. 'I'm sure he couldn't have done much to it. Look at your letter in the *Pell Mell*. Who wants more polish and refinement than that showed?'

'Ah, I didn't know you did me the honour of reading that.'

'Oh, yes; we both read it,' put in Mrs Wimp. 'I told Mr Wimp it was clever and cogent. After that quotation from the letter to the poor fellow's *fiancée* there could be no more doubt but that it was murder. Mr Wimp was convinced by it, too, weren't you, Edward?'

Edward coughed uneasily. It was a true statement, and therefore indiscreet. Grodman would plume himself terribly. At this moment Wimp felt that Grodman had been right in remaining a bachelor. Grodman perceived the humour of the situation, and wore a curious, sub-mocking smile.

'On the day I was born,' said Wimp's grandmother-in-law, 'over a hundred years ago, there was a babe murdered.' Wimp found himself wishing it had been she. He was anxious to get back to Cantercot. 'Don't let us talk shop on Christmas Day,' he said, smiling at Grodman. 'Besides, murder isn't a very appropriate subject.'

'No, it ain't,' said Grodman. 'How did we get on to it? Oh, yes—Denzil Cantercot. Ha! ha! ha! That's curious, for since Denzil wrote *Criminals I Have Caught*, his mind's running on nothing but murders. A poet's brain is easily turned.'

Wimp's eye glittered with excitement and contempt for Grodman's blindness. In Grodman's eye there danced an amused scorn of Wimp; to the outsider his amusement appeared at the expense of the poet.

Having wrought his rival up to the highest pitch, Grodman slyly and suddenly unstrung him.

'How lucky for Denzil!' he said, still in the same naïve, facetious Christmassy tone, 'that he can prove an alibi in this Constant affair.'

'An alibi!' gasped Wimp. 'Really?'

'Oh, yes. He was with his wife, you know. She's my woman of all work, Jane. She happened to mention his being with her.'

Jane had done nothing of the kind. After the colloquy he had overheard, Grodman had set himself to find out the relation between his two employees. By casually referring to Denzil as 'your husband', he so startled the poor woman that she did not attempt to deny the bond. Only once did he use the two words, but he was satisfied. As to the alibi he had not yet troubled her; but to take its existence for granted would upset and discomfort Wimp. For the moment that was triumph enough for Wimp's guest.

'Pa,' said Wilfred Wimp, 'what's a alleybi? A marble?'

'No, my lad,' said Grodman, 'it means being somewhere else when you're supposed to be somewhere.'

'Ah, playing truant,' said Wilfred self-consciously; his schoolmaster had often proved an alibi against him. 'Then Denzil will be hanged.'

Was it a prophecy? Wimp accepted it as such; as an oracle from the gods bidding him mistrust Grodman. Out of the mouths of little children issueth wisdom; sometimes even when they are not saying their lessons.

'When I was in my cradle, a century ago,' said Wimp's grandmother-in-law, 'men were hanged for stealing horses.'

They silenced her with snapdragon performances.

Wimp was busy thinking how to get at Grodman's factotum. Grodman was busy thinking how to get at Wimp's domestic. Neither received any of the usual messages from the Christmas Bells.

The next day was sloppy and uncertain. A thin rain drizzled languidly. One can stand that sort of thing on a summer Bank Holiday; one expects it. But to have a bad December Bank Holiday is too much of a bad thing. Some steps should surely be taken to confuse the weather clerk's chronology. Once let him know that Bank Holiday is coming, and he writes to the company for more water. Today his stock seemed low and he was dribbling it out; at times the wintry sun would shine in a feeble, diluted way, and though the holiday-makers would have preferred to take their sunshine neat, they swarmed forth in their myriads whenever there was a ray of hope. But it was only dodging the raindrops; up went the umbrellas again, and the streets became meadows of ambulating mushrooms.

Denzil Cantercot sat in his fur overcoat at the open window, looking at the landscape in water-colours. He smoked an after-dinner cigarette, and spoke of the Beautiful. Crowl was with him. They were in the first floor front, Crowl's bedroom, which, from its view of the Mile End Road, was livelier than the parlour with its outlook on the backyard. Mrs Crowl was an anti-tobacconist as regards the best bedroom; but Peter did not like to put the poet or his cigarette out. He felt there was something in common between smoke and poetry, over and above their being both Fads. Besides, Mrs Crowl was sulking in the kitchen. She had been arranging for an excursion with Peter and the children to Victoria Park. She had dreamed of the Crystal Palace, but Santa Claus had put no gifts in the cobbler's shoes. Now she could not risk spoiling the feather in her bonnet. The nine brats expressed their disappointment by slapping one another on the staircases. Peter felt that Mrs Crowl connected him in some way with the rainfall, and was unhappy. Was it not enough that he had been deprived of the pleasure of pointing out to a superstitious majority the mutual contradictions of Leviticus and the Song of Solomon? It was not often that Crowl could count on such an audience.

'And you still call Nature beautiful?' he said to Denzil, pointing to the ragged sky and the dripping eaves. 'Ugly old scarecrow!'

'Ugly she seems today,' admitted Denzil. 'But what is Ugliness but a higher form of Beauty? You have to look deeper into it to see it; such vision is the priceless gift of the few. To me this wan desolation of sighing rain is lovely as the sea-washed ruins of cities.'

'Ah, but you wouldn't like to go out in it,' said Peter Crowl. As he spoke the drizzle suddenly thickened into a torrent.

'We do not always kiss the woman we love.'

'Speak for yourself, Denzil. I'm only a plain man, and I want to know if Nature isn't a Fad. Hallo, there goes Mortlake! Lord, a minute of this will soak him to the skin.'

The labour leader was walking along with bowed head. He did not seem to mind the shower. It was some seconds before he even heard Crowl's invitation to him to take shelter. When he did hear it he shook his head.

'I know I can't offer you a drawing-room with duchesses stuck about it,' said Peter, vexed.

Tom turned the handle of the shop door and went in. There was nothing in the world which now galled him more than the suspicion that he was stuck-up and wished to cut old friends. He picked his way through the nine brats who clung affectionately to his wet knees, dispersing them finally by a jet of coppers to scramble for. Peter met him on the stairs and shook his hand lovingly and admiringly, and took him into Mrs Crowl's bedroom.

'Don't mind what I say, Tom. I'm only a plain man, and my tongue will say what comes uppermost! But it ain't from the soul, Tom, it ain't from the soul,' said Peter, punning feebly, and letting a mirthless smile play over his sallow features. 'You know Mr Cantercot, I suppose? The poet.'

'Oh, yes; how do you do, Tom? Seen the *New Pork Herald* lately? Not bad, those old times, eh?'

'No,' said Tom, 'I wish I was back in them.'

'Nonsense, nonsense,' said Peter, in much concern. 'Look at the good you are doing to the working man. Look how you are sweeping away the Fads. Ah, it's a grand thing to be gifted, Tom. The idea of your chuckin' yourself away on a composin' room! Manual labour is all very well for plain men like me, with no gift but just enough brains to see into the realities of things—to understand that we've got no soul and no immortality, and all that—and too selfish to look after anybody's comfort but my own and mother's and the kid's. But men like you and Cantercot—it ain't right that you should be peggin' away at low material things. Not that I think Cantercot's gospel's any value to the masses. The Beautiful is all very well for folks who've got nothing

else to think of, but give me the True. You're the man for
my money, Mortlake. No reference to the funds, Tom, to
which I contribute little enough, Heaven knows; though
how a *place* can know anything, Heaven alone knows. *You*
give us the Useful, Tom; that's what the world wants more
than the Beautiful.'

'Socrates said that the Useful *is* the Beautiful,' said Denzil.

'That may be,' said Peter, 'but the Beautiful ain't the Useful.'

'Nonsense!' said Denzil. 'What about Jessie—I mean Miss
Dymond? There's a combination for you. She always reminds
me of Grace Darling. How *is* she, Tom?'

'She's dead!' snapped Tom.

'What?' Denzil turned as white as a Christmas ghost.

'It was in the papers,' said Tom; 'all about her and the
lifeboat.'

'Oh, you mean Grace Darling,' said Denzil, visibly relieved.
'I meant Miss Dymond.'

'You needn't be so interested in her,' said Tom, surlily. 'She
don't appreciate it. Ah, the shower is over. I must be going.'

'No, stay a little longer, Tom,' pleaded Peter. 'I see a lot
about you in the papers, but very little of your dear old phiz
now. I can't spare the time to go and hear you. But I really
must give myself a treat. When's your next show?'

'Oh, I am always giving shows,' said Tom, smiling a little.
'But my next big performance is on the twenty-first of January,
when that picture of poor Mr Constant is to be unveiled at
the Bow Break o' Day Club. They have written to Gladstone
and other big pots to come down. I do hope the old man
accepts. A non-political gathering like this is the only occasion we could both speak at, and I have never been on the
same platform with Gladstone.'

He forgot his depression and ill-temper in the prospect,
and spoke with more animation.

'No, I should hope not, Tom,' said Peter. 'What with his
Fads about the Bible being a Rock, and Monarchy being the

right thing, he is a most dangerous man to lead the Radicals. He never lays his axe to the root of anything—except oak trees.'

'Mr Cantycot!' It was Mrs Crowl's voice that broke in upon the tirade. 'There's a *gentleman* to see you.' The astonishment Mrs Crowl put into the 'gentleman' was delightful. It was almost as good as a week's rent to her to give vent to her feelings. The controversial couple had moved away from the window when Tom entered, and had not noticed the immediate advent of another visitor who had spent his time profitably in listening to Mrs Crowl before asking to see the presumable object of his visit.

'Ask him up if it's a friend of yours, Cantercot,' said Peter. It was Wimp. Denzil was rather dubious as to the friendship, but he preferred to take Wimp diluted. 'Mortlake's upstairs,' he said. 'Will you come up and see him?'

Wimp had intended a duologue, but he made no objection, so he, too, stumbled through the nine brats to Mrs Crowl's bedroom. It was a queer quartet. Wimp had hardly expected to find anybody at the house on Boxing Day, but he did not care to waste a day. Was not Grodman, too, on the track? How lucky it was that Denzil had made the first overtures, so that he could approach him without exciting suspicion.

Mortlake scowled when he saw the detective. He objected to the police—on principle. But Crowl had no idea who the visitor was, even when told his name. He was rather pleased to meet one of Denzil's high-class friends, and welcomed him warmly. Probably he was some famous editor, which would account for his name stirring vague recollections. He summoned the eldest brat and sent him for beer (people would have their Fads), and not without trepidation called down to 'Mother' for glasses. 'Mother' observed at night (in the same apartment) that the beer money might have paid the week's school fees for half the family.

'We were just talking of poor Mr Constant's portrait, Mr Wimp,' said the unconscious Crowl; 'they're going to unveil it, Mortlake tells me, on the twenty-first of next month at the Bow Break o' Day Club.'

'Ah,' said Wimp, elated at being spared the trouble of manoeuvring the conversation; 'Mysterious affair that, Mr Crowl.'

'No; it's the right thing,' said Peter. 'There ought to be some memorial of the man in the district where he worked and where he died, poor chap.' The cobbler brushed away a tear.

'Yes, it's only right,' echoed Mortlake a whit eagerly. 'He was a noble fellow, a true philanthropist. The only thoroughly unselfish worker I've ever met.'

'He was that,' said Peter; 'and it's a rare pattern is unselfishness. Poor fellow, poor fellow. He preached the Useful, too. I've never met his like. Ah, I wish there was a Heaven for him to go to!' He blew his nose violently with a red pocket-handkerchief.

'Well, he's there, if there *is*,' said Tom.

'I hope he is,' added Wimp fervently; 'but I shouldn't like to go there the way he did.'

'You were the last person to see him, Tom, weren't you?' said Denzil.

'Oh, no,' answered Tom quickly. 'You remember he went out after me; at least, so Mrs Drabdump said at the inquest.'

'That last conversation he had with you, Tom,' said Denzil. 'He didn't say anything to you that would lead you to suppose—'

'No, of course not!' interrupted Mortlake impatiently.

'Do you really think he was murdered, Tom?' said Denzil.

'Mr Wimp's opinion on that point is more valuable than mine,' replied Tom, testily. 'It may have been suicide. Men often get sick of life—especially if they are bored,' he added meaningly.

'Ah, but you were the last person known to be with him,' said Denzil.

Crowl laughed. 'Had you there, Tom.'

But they did not have Tom there much longer, for he

departed, looking even worse-tempered than when he came. Wimp went soon after, and Crowl and Denzil were left to their interminable argumentation concerning the Useful and the Beautiful.

Wimp went West. He had several strings (or cords) to his bow, and he ultimately found himself at Kensal Green Cemetery. Being there, he went down the avenues of the dead to a grave to note down the exact date of a death. It was a day on which the dead seemed enviable. The dull, sodden sky, the dripping, leafless trees, the wet spongy soil, the reeking grass—everything combined to make one long to be in a warm, comfortable grave, away from the leaden *ennuis* of life. Suddenly the detective's keen eye caught sight of a figure that made his heart throb with sudden excitement. It was that of a woman in a grey shawl and a brown bonnet standing before a railed-in grave. She had no umbrella. The rain plashed mournfully upon her, but left no trace on her soaking garments. Wimp crept up behind her, but she paid no heed to him. Her eyes were lowered to the grave, which seemed to be drawing them toward it by some strange morbid fascination. His eyes followed hers. The simple headstone bore the name: 'ARTHUR CONSTANT'.

Wimp tapped her suddenly on the shoulder. 'How do you do, Mrs Drabdump?'

Mrs Drabdump went deadly white. She turned round, staring at Wimp without any recognition.

'You remember me, surely,' he said. 'I've been down once or twice to your place about that poor gentleman's papers.' His eye indicated the grave.

'Lor! I remember you now,' said Mrs Drabdump.

'Won't you come under my umbrella? You must be drenched to the skin.'

'It don't matter, sir. I can't take no hurt. I've had the rheumatics this twenty year.'

Mrs Drabdump shrank from accepting Wimp's attentions,

not so much perhaps because he was a man as because he was a gentleman. Mrs Drabdump liked to see the fine folks keep their place, and not contaminate their skirts by contact with the lower castes. 'It's set wet, it'll rain right into the new year,' she announced. 'And they say a bad beginnin' makes a worse endin'.' Mrs Drabdump was one of those persons who give you the idea that they just missed being born barometers.

'But what are you doing in this miserable spot, so far from home?' queried the detective.

'It's Bank Holiday,' Mrs Drabdump reminded him in tones of acute surprise. 'I always make a hexcursion on Bank Holiday.'

CHAPTER VIII

THE New Year brought Mrs Drabdump a new lodger. He was an old gentleman with a long grey beard. He rented the rooms of the late Mr Constant, and lived a very retired life. Haunted rooms—or rooms that ought to be haunted if the ghosts of those murdered in them had any self-respect—are supposed to fetch a lower rent in the market. The whole Irish problem might be solved if the spirits of 'Mr Balfour's victims' would only depreciate the value of property to a point consistent with the support of an agricultural population. But Mrs Drabdump's new lodger paid so much for his rooms that he laid himself open to a suspicion of special interest in ghosts. Perhaps he was a member of the Psychical Society. The neighbourhood imagined him another mad philanthropist, but as he did not appear to be doing any good to anybody it relented and conceded his sanity. Mortlake, who occasionally stumbled across him in the passage, did not trouble himself to think about him at all. He was too full of other troubles and cares. Though he worked harder than ever, the spirit seemed to have gone out of him. Sometimes he forgot himself in a fine rapture of eloquence—lashing himself up into a divine resentment of injustice or a passion of sympathy with the sufferings of his brethren—but mostly he plodded on in dull, mechanical fashion. He still made brief provincial tours, starring a day here and a day there, and everywhere his admirers remarked how jaded and overworked he looked. There was talk of starting a subscription to give him a holiday on the Continent—a luxury obviously unobtainable on the few pounds allowed him per week. The new lodger would doubtless have been pleased to subscribe, for he seemed quite to like occupying Mortlake's chamber the nights he was absent, though he was thoughtful enough not to disturb the hard-worked landlady in the adjoining room by unseemly noise. Wimp was always a quiet man.

Meantime the 21st of the month approached, and the East End was in excitement. Mr Gladstone had consented to be present at the ceremony of unveiling the portrait of Arthur Constant, presented by an unknown donor to the Bow Break o' Day Club, and it was to be a great function. The whole affair was outside the lines of party politics, so that even Conservatives and Socialists considered themselves justified in pestering the committee for tickets. To say nothing of ladies. As the committee desired to be present themselves, nine-tenths of the applications for admission had to be refused, as is usual on these occasions. The committee agreed among themselves to exclude the fair sex altogether as the only way of disposing of their womankind who were making speeches as long as Mr Gladstone's. Each committeeman told his sisters, female cousins and aunts that the other committeemen had insisted on divesting the function of all grace; and what could a man do when he was in a minority of one?

Crowl, who was not a member of the Break o' Day Club, was particularly anxious to hear the great orator whom he despised; fortunately Mortlake remembered the cobbler's anxiety to hear himself, and on the eve of the ceremony sent him a ticket. Crowl was in the first flush of possession when Denzil Cantercot returned, after a sudden and unannounced absence of three days. His clothes were muddy and tattered, his cocked hat was deformed, his cavalier beard was matted, and his eyes were bloodshot. The cobbler nearly dropped the ticket at the sight of him. 'Hullo, Cantercot!' he gasped. 'Why, where have you been all these days?'

'Terribly busy!' said Denzil. 'Here, give me a glass of water. I'm dry as the Sahara.'

Crowl ran inside and got the water, trying hard not to inform Mrs Crowl of their lodger's return. 'Mother' had expressed herself freely on the subject of the poet during his absence, and not in terms which would have commended themselves to the poet's fastidious literary sense. Indeed, she did not hesitate to call him a sponger and a low swindler, who had run away to avoid paying the piper. Her fool of a husband might be quite sure he would never set eyes on the scoundrel again. However, Mrs Crowl was wrong. Here was Denzil back again. And yet Mr Crowl felt no sense of victory. He had no desire to crow over his partner and to utter that 'See! didn't I tell you so?' which is a greater consolation than religion in most of the misfortunes of life. Unfortunately, to get the water, Crowl had to go to the kitchen; and as he was usually such a temperate man, this desire for drink in the middle of the day attracted the attention of the lady in possession. Crowl had to explain the situation. Mrs Crowl ran into the shop to improve it. Mr Crowl followed in dismay, leaving a trail of spilled water in his wake.

'You good-for-nothing, disreputable scarecrow, where have—'

'Hush, mother. Let him drink. Mr Cantercot is thirsty.'

'Does he care if my children are hungry?'

Denzil tossed the water greedily down his throat almost at a gulp, as if it were brandy.

'Madam,' he said, smacking his lips, 'I do care. I care intensely. Few things in life would grieve me more deeply than to hear that a child, a dear little child—the Beautiful in a nutshell—had suffered hunger. You wrong me.' His voice was tremulous with the sense of injury. Tears stood in his eyes.

'Wrong you? I've no wish to *wrong* you,' said Mrs Crowl. 'I should like to *hang* you.'

'Don't talk of such ugly things,' said Denzil, touching his throat nervously.

'Well, what have you been doin' all this time?'

'Why, what should I be doing?'

'How should I know what became of you? I thought it was another murder.'

'What!' Denzil's glass dashed to fragments on the floor. 'What do you mean?'

But Mrs Crowl was glaring too viciously at Mr Crowl to reply. He understood the message as if it were printed. It ran: 'You have broken one of my best glasses. You have annihilated threepence, or a week's school fees for half the family.' Peter wished she would turn the lightning upon Denzil, a conductor down whom it would run innocuously. He stooped down and picked up the pieces as carefully as if they were cuttings from the Koh-i-noor. Thus the lightning passed harmlessly over his head and flew toward Cantercot.

'What do I mean?' Mrs Crowl echoed, as if there had been no interval. 'I mean that it would be a good thing if you *had* been murdered.'

'What unbeautiful ideas you have, to be sure!' murmured Denzil.

'Yes; but they'd be useful,' said Mrs Crowl, who had not lived with Peter all these years for nothing. 'And if you haven't been murdered what *have* you been doing?'

'My dear, my dear,' put in Crowl, deprecatingly, looking up from his quadrupedal position like a sad dog, 'you are not Cantercot's keeper.'

'Oh, ain't I?' flashed his spouse. 'Who else keeps him, I should like to know?'

Peter went on picking up the pieces of the Koh-i-noor.

'I have no secrets from Mrs Crowl,' Denzil explained courteously. 'I have been working day and night bringing out a new paper. Haven't had a wink of sleep for three nights.'

Peter looked up at his bloodshot eyes with respectful interest.

'The capitalist met me in the street—an old friend of mine—I was overjoyed at the *rencontre* and told him the Idea I'd been brooding over for months and he promised to stand all the racket.'

'What sort of a paper?' said Peter.

'Can you ask? To what do you think I've been devoting my days and nights but to the cultivation of the Beautiful?'

'Is that what the paper will be devoted to?'

'Yes. To the Beautiful.'

'I know,' snorted Mrs Crowl, 'with portraits of actresses.'

'Portraits? Oh, no!' said Denzil. 'That would be the True—not the Beautiful.'

'And what's the name of the paper?' asked Crowl.

'Ah, that's a secret, Peter. Like Scott, I prefer to remain anonymous.'

'Just like your Fads. I'm only a plain man, and I want to know where the fun of anonymity comes in? If I had any gifts, I should like to get the credit. It's a right and natural feeling, to my thinking.'

'Unnatural, Peter; unnatural. We're all born anonymous, and I'm for sticking close to Nature. Enough for me that I disseminate the Beautiful. Any letters come during my absence, Mrs Crowl?'

'No,' she snapped. 'But a gent named Grodman called. He said you hadn't been to see him for some time, and looked annoyed to hear you'd disappeared. How much have you let *him* in for?'

'The man's in *my* debt,' said Denzil, annoyed. 'I wrote a book for him and he's taken all the credit for it, the rogue! My name doesn't appear even in the Preface. What's that ticket you're looking so lovingly at, Peter?'

'That's for tonight—the unveiling of Constant's portrait. Gladstone speaks. Awful demand for places.'

'Gladstone!' sneered Denzil. 'Who wants to hear Gladstone? A man who's devoted his life to pulling down the pillars of Church and State.'

'A man's who's devoted his whole life to propping up the crumbling Fads of Religion and Monarchy. But, for all that, the man has his gifts, and I'm burnin' to hear him.'

'I wouldn't go out of my way an inch to hear him,' said Denzil; and went up to his room, and when Mrs Crowl sent him up a cup of nice strong tea at tea time, the brat who bore it found him lying dressed on the bed, snoring unbeautifully.

The evening wore on. It was fine frosty weather. The Whitechapel Road swarmed, with noisy life, as though it were a Saturday night. The stars flared in the sky like the lights of celestial costermongers. Everybody was on the alert for the advent of Mr Gladstone. He must surely come through the Road on his journey from the West Bow-wards. But nobody saw him or his carriage, except those about the Hall. Probably he went by tram most of the way. He would have caught cold in an open carriage, or bobbing his head out of the window of a closed.

'If he had only been a German prince, or a cannibal king,' said Crowl bitterly, as he plodded toward the Club, 'we should have disguised Mile End in bunting and blue fire. But perhaps it's a compliment. He knows his London, and it's no use trying to hide the facts from him. They must have queer notions of cities, those monarchs. They must fancy everybody lives in a flutter of flags and walks about under triumphal arches, like as if I were to stitch shoes in my Sunday clothes.' By a defiance of chronology Crowl had them on today, and they seemed to accentuate the simile.

'And why shouldn't life be fuller of the Beautiful,' said Denzil. The poet had brushed the reluctant mud off his garments to the extent it was willing to go, and had washed his face, but his eyes were still bloodshot from the cultivation of the Beautiful. Denzil was accompanying Crowl to the door of the Club out of good fellowship. Denzil was himself accompanied by Grodman, though less obtrusively. Least obtrusively was he accompanied by his usual Scotland Yard shadows, Wimp's agents. There was a surging nondescript crowd about the Club, and the police, and the doorkeeper, and the stewards could with difficulty keep out the tide of the ticketless, through which the current of the privileged had equal difficulty in permeating. The streets all around were thronged with people longing for a glimpse of Gladstone. Mortlake drove up in a hansom (his head a self-conscious pendulum of popularity, swaying and bowing to right and left) and received all the pent-up enthusiasm.

'Well, good-bye, Cantercot,' said Crowl.

'No, I'll see you to the door, Peter.'

They fought their way shoulder to shoulder.

Now that Grodman had found Denzil he was not going to lose him again. He had only found him by accident, for he was himself bound to the unveiling ceremony, to which he had been invited in view of his known devotion to the task of unveiling the Mystery. He spoke to one of the policemen about, who said, 'Ay, ay, sir,' and he was prepared to follow Denzil, if necessary, and to give up the pleasure of hearing Gladstone for an acuter thrill. The arrest must be delayed no longer.

But Denzil seemed as if he were going in on the heels of Crowl. This would suit Grodman better. He could then have the two pleasures. But Denzil was stopped half-way through the door.

'Ticket, sir!'

Denzil drew himself up to his full height.

'Press,' he said, majestically. All the glories and grandeurs of the Fourth Estate were concentrated in that haughty monosyllable. Heaven itself is full of journalists who have overawed St Peter. But the doorkeeper was a veritable dragon.

'What paper, sir?'

'*New Pork Herald*,' said Denzil sharply. He did not relish his word being distrusted.

'*New York Herald*,' said one of the bystanding stewards, scarce catching the sounds. 'Pass him in.'

And in the twinkling of an eye, Denzil had eagerly slipped inside.

But during the brief altercation Wimp had come up. Even he could not make his face quite impassive, and there was a suppressed intensity in the eyes and a quiver about the mouth. He went in on Denzil's heels, blocking up the doorway with Grodman. The two men were so full of their coming *coups* that they struggled for some seconds, side by side, before they recognized each other. Then they shook hands heartily.

'That was Cantercot just went in, wasn't it, Grodman?' said Wimp.

'I didn't notice,' said Grodman, in tones of utter indifference.

At bottom Wimp was terribly excited. He felt that his *coup* was going to be executed under very sensational circumstances. Everything would combine to turn the eyes of the country upon him—nay, of the world, for had not the Big Bow Mystery been discussed in every language under the sun? In these electric times the criminal achieves a cosmopolitan reputation. It is a privilege he shares with few other artists. This time Wimp would be one of them; and, he felt, deservedly so. If the criminal had been cunning to the point of genius in planning the murder, he had been acute to the point of divination in detecting it. Never before had he pieced together so broken a chain. He could not resist the unique opportunity of setting a sensational scheme in a sensational framework. The dramatic instinct was strong in him; he felt like a playwright who has constructed a strong melodramatic plot, and has the Drury Lane stage suddenly offered him to present it on. It would be folly to deny himself the luxury, though the presence of Mr Gladstone and the nature of the ceremony should perhaps have given him pause. Yet, on the other hand, these were the very factors of the temptation. Wimp went in and took a seat behind Denzil. All the seats were numbered, so that everybody might have the satisfaction of occupying somebody else's. Denzil was in the special reserved places in the front row just by the central gangway; Crowl was squeezed into a corner behind a pillar near the back of the hall. Grodman had been honoured with a seat on the platform, which was accessible by steps on the right and left, but he kept his eye on Denzil. The picture of the poor idealist hung on the wall behind Grodman's head, covered by its curtain of brown holland. There was a subdued buzz of excitement about the hall, which swelled into cheers every now and again as some gentleman known to fame or Bow took his place upon the platform. It was occupied by several local M.P.s of varying politics, a number of other Parliamentary satellites of the great man, three or four labour leaders, a peer or two of philanthropic pretensions, a sprinkling of Toynbee and Oxford Hall men, the president and other honorary officials, some of the family and friends of the deceased, together with the inevitable percentage of persons who had no claim to be there save cheek. Gladstone was late—later than Mortlake, who was cheered to the echo when he arrived, someone starting 'For He's a Jolly Good Fellow' as if it were a political meeting. Gladstone came in just in time to acknowledge the compliment. The noise of the song, trolled out from iron lungs, had drowned the huzzahs heralding the old man's advent. The convivial chorus went to Mortlake's head, as if champagne had really preceded it. His eyes grew moist and dim. He saw himself swimming to the Millennium on waves of enthusiasm. Ah, how his brother toilers should be rewarded for their trust in him!

With his usual courtesy and consideration, Mr Gladstone had refused to perform the actual unveiling of Arthur Constant's portrait. 'That,' he said in his postcard, 'will fall most appropriately to Mr Mortlake, a gentleman who has, I am given to understand, enjoyed the personal friendship of the late Mr Constant, and has co-operated with him in various schemes for the organization of skilled and unskilled classes of labour, as well as for the diffusion of better ideals—ideals of self-culture and self-restraint—among the working-men of Bow, who have been fortunate, so far as I can perceive, in the possession (if in one case unhappily only temporary posses-sion) of two such men of undoubted ability and honesty to direct their divided counsels and to lead them along a road, which, though I cannot pledge myself to approve of it in all its turnings and windings, is yet not unfitted to bring them somewhat nearer to goals to which there are few of us but would extend some measure of hope that the working classes of this great Empire may in due course, yet with no unnecessary delay, be enabled to arrive.'

Mr Gladstone's speech was an expansion of his postcard, punctuated by cheers. The only new thing in it was the graceful and touching way in which he revealed what had been a secret up till then—that the portrait had been painted and presented to the Bow Break o' Day Club by Lucy Brent, who in the fulness of time would have been Arthur Constant's wife. It was a painting for which he had sat to her while alive, and she had stifled yet pampered her grief by working hard at it since his death. The fact added the last touch of pathos to the occasion. Crowl's face was hidden behind his red handkerchief; even the fire of excitement in Wimp's eye was quenched for a moment by a tear-drop, as he thought of Mrs Wimp and Wilfred. As for Grodman, there was almost a lump in his throat. Denzil Cantercot was the only unmoved man in the room. He thought the episode quite too Beautiful, and was already weaving it into rhyme.

At the conclusion of his speech Mr Gladstone called upon Tom Mortlake to unveil the portrait. Tom rose, pale and excited. His hand faltered as he touched the cord. He seemed overcome with emotion. Was it the mention of Lucy Brent that had moved him to his depths?

The brown holland fell away—the dead stood revealed as he had been in life. Every feature, painted by the hand of Love, was instinct with vitality: the fine, earnest face, the sad kindly eyes, the noble brow seeming still a-throb with the thought of Humanity. A thrill ran through the room—there was a low, undefinable murmur. O, the pathos and the tragedy of it! Every eye was fixed, misty with emotion, upon the dead man in the picture and the living man who stood, pale and agitated, and visibly unable to commence his speech, at the side of the canvas. Suddenly a hand was laid upon the labour leader's shoulder, and there rang through the hall in Wimp's clear, decisive tones the words: 'Tom Mortlake, I arrest you for the murder of Arthur Constant!'

CHAPTER IX

FOR a moment there was an acute, terrible silence. Mortlake's face was that of a corpse; the face of the dead man at his side was flushed with the hues of life. To the overstrung nerves of the onlookers, the brooding eyes of the picture seemed sad and stern with menace, and charged with the lightnings of doom.

It was a horrible contrast. For Wimp, alone, the painted face had fuller, more tragical, meanings. The audience seemed turned to stone. They sat or stood—in every variety of attitude—frozen, rigid. Arthur Constant's picture dominated the scene, the only living thing in a hall of the dead.

But only for a moment. Mortlake shook off the detective's hand.

'Boys!' he cried, in accents of infinite indignation, 'this is a police conspiracy.'

His words relaxed the tension. The stony figures were agitated. A dull, excited hubbub answered him. The little cobbler darted from behind his pillar, and leaped upon a bench. The cords of his brow were swollen with excitement. He seemed a giant overshadowing the hall.

'Boys!' he roared, in his best Victoria Park voice, 'listen to me. This charge is a foul and damnable lie.'

'Bravo!' 'Hear, hear!' 'Hooray!' 'It is!' was roared back at him from all parts of the room. Everybody rose and stood in tentative attitudes, excited to the last degree.

'Boys!' Peter roared on, 'you all know me. I'm a plain man, and I want to know if it's likely a man would murder his best friend.'

'No!' in a mighty volume of sound.

Wimp had scarcely calculated upon Mortlake's popularity. He stood on the platform, pale and anxious as his prisoner.

'And if he did, why didn't they prove it the first time?'

'HEAR, HEAR!'

'And if they want to arrest him, why couldn't they leave it till the ceremony was over? Tom Mortlake's not the man to run away.'

'Tom Mortlake! Tom Mortlake! Three cheers for Tom Mortlake! Hip, hip, hip, hooray!'

'Three groans for the police.' 'Hoo! Oo! Oo!'

Wimp's melodrama was not going well. He felt like the author to whose ears is borne the ominous sibilance of the pit. He almost wished he had not followed the curtain-raiser with his own stronger drama. Unconsciously the police, scattered about the hall, drew together. The people on the platform knew not what to do. They had all risen and stood in a densely-packed mass. Even Mr Gladstone's speech failed him in circumstances so novel. The groans died away; the cheers for Mortlake rose and swelled and fell and rose again. Sticks and umbrellas were banged and rattled, handkerchiefs were waved, the thunder deepened. The motley crowd still surging about the hall took up the cheers, and for hundreds of yards around people were going black in the face out of mere irresponsible enthusiasm. At last Tom waved his hand—the thunder dwindled, died. The prisoner was master of the situation.

Grodman stood on the platform, grasping the back of his chair, a curious mocking Mephistophelian glitter about his eyes, his lips wreathed into a half smile. There was no hurry for him to get Denzil Cantercot arrested now. Wimp had made an egregious, colossal blunder. In Grodman's heart there was a great glad calm as of a man who has strained his sinews to win in a famous match, and has heard the judge's word. He felt almost kindly to Denzil now.

Tom Mortlake spoke. His face was set and stony. His tall figure was drawn up haughtily to its full height. He pushed the black mane back from his forehead with a characteristic gesture. The fevered audience hung upon his lips—the men at the back leaned eagerly forward—the reporters were breathless with fear lest they should miss a word. What would the great labour leader have to say at this supreme moment?

'Mr Chairman and Gentlemen: It is to me a melancholy pleasure to have been honoured with the task of unveiling tonight this portrait of a great benefactor to Bow and a true friend to the labouring classes. Except that he honoured me with his friendship while living, and that the aspirations of my life have, in my small and restricted way, been identical with his, there is little reason why this honourable duty should have fallen upon me. Gentlemen, I trust that we shall all find an inspiring influence in the daily vision of the dead, who yet liveth in our hearts and in this noble work of art—wrought, as Mr Gladstone has told us, by the hand of one who loved him.' The speaker paused a moment, his low vibrant tones faltering into silence. 'If we humble working-men of Bow can never hope to exert individually a tithe of the beneficial influence wielded by Arthur Constant, it is yet possible for each of us to walk in the light he has kindled in our midst—a perpetual lamp of self-sacrifice and brotherhood.'

That was all. The room rang with cheers. Tom Mortlake resumed his seat. To Wimp the man's audacity verged on the Sublime; to Denzil on the Beautiful. Again there was a breathless hush. Mr Gladstone's mobile face was working with excitement. No such extraordinary scene had occurred in the whole of his extraordinary experience. He seemed about to rise. The cheering subsided to a painful stillness. Wimp cut the situation by laying his hand again upon Tom's shoulder.

'Come quietly with me,' he said. The words were almost a whisper, but in the supreme silence they travelled to the ends of the hall.

'Don't you go, Tom!' The trumpet tones were Peter's. The call thrilled an answering chord of defiance in every breast, and a low, ominous murmur swept through the hall.

Tom rose, and there was silence again. 'Boys,' he said, 'let me go. Don't make any noise about it. I shall be with you again tomorrow.'

But the blood of the Break o' Day boys was at fever heat. A hurtling mass of men struggled confusedly from their seats. In a moment all was chaos. Tom did not move. Half-a-dozen men, headed by Peter, scaled the platform. Wimp was thrown to one side, and the invaders formed a ring round Tom's chair. The platform people scampered like mice from the centre. Some huddled together in the corners, others slipped out at the rear. The committee congratulated themselves on having had the self-denial to exclude ladies. Mr Gladstone's satellites hurried the old man off and into his carriage; though the fight promised to become Homeric. Grodman stood at the side of the platform secretly more amused than ever, concerning himself no more with Denzil Cantercot, who was already strengthening his nerves at the bar upstairs. The police about the hall blew their whistles, and policemen came rushing in from outside and the neighbourhood. An Irish M.P. on the platform was waving his gingham like a shillelagh in sheer excitement, forgetting his new-found respectability and dreaming himself back at Donnybrook Fair. Him a conscientious constable floored with a truncheon. But a shower of fists fell on the zealot's face, and he tottered back bleeding. Then the storm broke in all its fury. The upper air was black with staves, sticks, and umbrellas, mingled with the pallid hailstones of knobby fists. Yells and groans and hoots and battle-cries blent in grotesque chorus, like one of Dvorák's weird diabolical movements. Mortlake stood impassive, with arms folded, making no further effort, and the battle raged round him as the water swirls around some steadfast rock. A posse of police from the back fought their way steadily toward him, and charged up the heights of the platform steps, only to be sent tumbling backward, as their leader was hurled at them like a battering ram. Upon the top of the heap fell he, surmounting the strata of policemen. But others clambered upon them, escalading the platform. A moment more and Mortlake would have been taken, after being well shaken. Then the miracle happened.

As when of old a reputable goddess *ex machina* saw her favourite hero in dire peril, straightway she drew down a cloud from the celestial stores of Jupiter and enveloped her fondling in kindly night, so that his adversary strove with the darkness, so did Crowl, the cunning cobbler, the much-daring, essay to insure his friend's safety. He turned off the gas at the meter.

An Arctic night—unpreceded by twilight—fell, and there dawned the sabbath of the witches. The darkness could be felt—and it left blood and bruises behind it. When the lights were turned on again, Mortlake was gone. But several of the rioters were arrested, triumphantly.

And through all, and over all, the face of the dead man who had sought to bring peace on earth, brooded.

Crowl sat meekly eating his supper of bread and cheese, with his head bandaged, while Denzil Cantercot told him the story of how he had rescued Tom Mortlake. He had been among the first to scale the height, and had never budged from Tom's side or from the forefront of the battle till he had seen him safely outside and into a by-street.

'I am so glad you saw that he got away safely,' said Crowl, 'I wasn't quite sure he would.'

'Yes; but I wish some cowardly fool hadn't turned off the gas. I like men to see that they are beaten.'

'But it seemed—easier,' faltered Crowl.

'Easier!' echoed Denzil, taking a deep draught of bitter. 'Really, Peter, I'm sorry to find you always will take such low views. It may be easier, but it's shabby. It shocks one's sense of the Beautiful.'

Crowl ate his bread and cheese shamefacedly.

'But what was the use of breaking your head to save him?' said Mrs Crowl with an unconscious pun. 'He must be caught.'

'Ah, I don't see how the Useful *does* come in, now,' said Peter thoughtfully. 'But I didn't think of that at the time.'

He swallowed his water quickly and it went the wrong way and added to his confusion. It also began to dawn upon him that he might be called to account. Let it be said at once that he wasn't. He had taken too prominent a part.

Meantime, Mrs Wimp was bathing Mr Wimp's eye, and rubbing him generally with arnica. Wimp's melodrama had been, indeed, a sight for the gods. Only, virtue was vanquished and vice triumphant. The villain had escaped, and without striking a blow.

CHAPTER X

THERE was matter and to spare for the papers the next day. The striking ceremony—Mr Gladstone's speech—the sensational arrest—these would of themselves have made excellent themes for reports and leaders. But the personality of the man arrested, and the Big Bow Mystery Battle—as it came to be called—gave additional piquancy to the paragraphs and the posters. The behaviour of Mortlake put the last touch to the picturesqueness of the position. He left the hall when the lights went out, and walked unnoticed and unmolested through pleiads of policemen to the nearest police station, where the superintendent was almost too excited to take any notice of his demand to be arrested. But to do him justice, the official yielded as soon as he understood the situation. It seems inconceivable that he did not violate some red-tape regulation in so doing. To some this self-surrender was limpid proof of innocence; to others it was the damning token of despairing guilt.

The morning papers were pleasant reading for Grodman, who chuckled as continuously over his morning egg, as if he had laid it. Jane was alarmed for the sanity of her saturnine master. As her husband would have said, Grodman's grins were not Beautiful. But he made no effort to suppress them. Not only had Wimp perpetrated a grotesque blunder, but the journalists to a man were down on his great sensation tableau, though their denunciations did not appear in the dramatic columns. The Liberal papers said that he had endangered Mr Gladstone's life; the Conservative that he had unloosed the raging elements of Bow blackguardism, and set in motion forces which might have easily swelled to a riot, involving severe destruction of property. But 'Tom Mortlake' was, after all, the thought swamping every other. It was, in a sense, a triumph for the man.

But Wimp's turn came when Mortlake, who reserved his defence, was brought up before a magistrate and, by force of the new evidence, fully committed for trial on the charge of murdering Arthur Constant. Then men's thoughts centred again on the Mystery, and the solution of the inexplicable problem agitated mankind from China to Peru.

In the middle of February, the great trial befell. It was another of the opportunities which the Chancellor of the Exchequer neglects. So stirring a drama might have easily cleared its expenses—despite the length of the cast, the salaries of the stars, and the rent of the house—in mere advance booking. For it was a drama which (by the rights of Magna Charta) could never be repeated; a drama which ladies of fashion would have given their earrings to witness, even with the central figure not a woman. And there *was* a woman in it anyhow, to judge by the little that had transpired at the magisterial examination, and the fact that the country was placarded with bills offering a reward for information concerning a Miss Jessie Dymond. Mortlake was defended by Sir Charles Brown-Harland, Q.C., retained at the expense of the Mortlake Defence Fund (subscriptions to which came also from Australia and the Continent), and set on his mettle by the fact that he was the accepted labour candidate for an East-end constituency. Their Majesties, Victoria and the Law, were represented by Mr Robert Spigot, Q.C.

MR SPIGOT, Q.C., in presenting his case, said: 'I propose to show that the prisoner murdered his friend and fellow-lodger, Mr Arthur Constant, in cold blood, and with the most careful premeditation; premeditation so studied, as to leave the circumstances of the death an impenetrable mystery for weeks to all the world, though fortunately without altogether baffling the almost superhuman ingenuity of Mr Edward Wimp, of the Scotland Yard Detective Department. I propose to show that the motives of the prisoner were jealousy and revenge; jealousy not only of his friend's superior influence over the working-men he himself aspired to lead, but the more commonplace animosity engendered by the disturbing element of a woman having relations to both. If, before my case is complete, it will be my painful duty to show that the murdered man was not the saint the world has agreed to paint him, I shall not shrink from unveiling the truer picture, in the interests of justice, which cannot say *nil nisi bonum* even of the dead. I propose to show that the murder was committed by the prisoner shortly before half-past six on the morning of December 4th, and that the prisoner having, with the remarkable ingenuity which he has shown throughout, attempted to prepare an alibi by feigning to leave London by the *first* train to Liverpool, returned home, got in with his latchkey through the street-door, which he had left on the latch, unlocked his victim's bedroom with a key which he possessed, cut the sleeping man's throat, pocketed his razor, locked the door again, and gave it the appearance of being bolted, went downstairs, unslipped the bolt of the big lock, closed the door behind him, and got to Euston in time for the *second* train to Liverpool. The fog helped his proceedings throughout.' Such was in sum the theory of the prosecution. The pale defiant figure in the dock winced perceptibly under parts of it.

Mrs Drabdump was the first witness called for the prosecution. She was quite used to legal inquisitiveness by this time, but did not appear in good spirits.

'On the night of December 3rd, you gave the prisoner a letter?'

'Yes, your ludship.'

'How did he behave when he read it?'

'He turned very pale and excited. He went up to the poor gentleman's room, and I'm afraid he quarrelled with him. He might have left his last hours peaceful.' (*Amusement.*)

'What happened then?'

'Mr Mortlake went out in a passion, and came in again in about an hour.'

'He told you he was going away to Liverpool very early the next morning.'

'No, your ludship, he said he was going to Devonport.' (*Sensation.*)

'What time did you get up the next morning?'

'Half-past six.'

'That is not your usual time?'

'No, I always get up at six.'

'How do you account for the extra sleepiness?'

'Misfortunes will happen.'

'It wasn't the dull, foggy weather?'

'No, my lud, else I should never get up early.' (*Laughter.*)

'You drink something before going to bed?'

'I like my cup o' tea. I take it strong, without sugar. It always steadies my nerves.'

'Quite so. Where were you when the prisoner told you he was going to Devonport?'

'Drinkin' my tea in the kitchen.'

'What should you say if prisoner dropped something in it to make you sleep late?'

WITNESS (*startled*): 'He ought to be shot.'

'He might have done it without your noticing it, I suppose?'

'If he was clever enough to murder the poor gentleman, he was clever enough to try and poison me.'

THE JUDGE: 'The witness in her replies must confine herself to the evidence.'

MR SPIGOT, Q.C.: 'I must submit to your lordship that it is a very logical answer, and exactly illustrates the interdependence of the probabilities. Now, Mrs Drabdump, let us know what happened when you awoke at half-past six the next morning.'

Thereupon Mrs Drabdump recapitulated the evidence (with new redundancies, but slight variations) given by her at the inquest. How she became alarmed—how she found the street-door locked by the big lock—how she roused Grodman, and got him to burst open the door—how they found the body—all this with which the public was already familiar *ad nauseam* was extorted from her afresh.

'Look at this key' (key passed to the witness). 'Do you recognize it?'

'Yes; how did you get it? It's the key of my first-floor front. I am sure I left it sticking in the door.'

'Did you know a Miss Dymond?'

'Yes, Mr Mortlake's sweetheart. But I knew he would never marry her, poor thing.' (*Sensation.*)

'Why not?'

'He was getting too grand for her.' (*Amusement.*)

'You don't mean anything more than that?'

'I don't know; she only came to my place once or twice. The last time I set eyes on her must have been in October.'

'How did she appear?'

'She was very miserable, but she wouldn't let you see it.' (*Laughter.*)

'How has the prisoner behaved since the murder?'

'He always seemed very glum and sorry for it.'

Cross-examined: 'Did not the prisoner once occupy the bedroom of Mr Constant, and give it up to him, so that Mr Constant might have the two rooms on the same floor?'

'Yes, but he didn't pay as much.'

'And, while occupying this front bedroom, did not the prisoner once lose his key and have another made?'

'He did; he was very careless.'

'Do you know what the prisoner and Mr Constant spoke about on the night of December 3rd?'

'No; I couldn't hear.'

'Then how did you know they were quarrelling?'

'They were talkin' so loud.'

Sir Charles Brown-Harland, Q.C. (*sharply*): 'But I'm talking loudly to you now. Should you say I was quarrelling?'

'It takes two to make a quarrel.' (*Laughter.*)

'Was the prisoner the sort of man who, in your opinion, would commit a murder?'

'No, I never should ha' guessed it was him.'

'He always struck you as a thorough gentleman?'

'No, my lud. I knew he was only a comp.'

'You say the prisoner has seemed depressed since the murder. Might not that have been due to the disappearance of his sweetheart?'

'No, he'd more likely be glad to get rid of her.'

'Then he wouldn't be jealous if Mr Constant took her off his hands?' (*Sensation.*)

'Men are dog-in-the-mangers.'

'Never mind about men, Mrs Drabdump. Had the prisoner ceased to care for Miss Dymond?'

'He didn't seem to think of her, my lud. When he got a letter in her handwriting among his heap he used to throw it aside till he'd torn open the others.'

BROWN-HARLAND, Q.C. (*with a triumphant ring in his voice*): 'Thank you, Mrs Drabdump. You may sit down.'

SPIGOT, Q.C.: 'One moment, Mrs Drabdump. You say the prisoner had ceased to care for Miss Dymond. Might not this have been in consequence of his suspecting for some time that she had relations with Mr Constant?'

THE JUDGE: 'That is not a fair question.'

SPIGOT, Q.C.: 'That will do, thank you, Mrs Drabdump.'

BROWN-HARLAND, Q.C.: 'No; one question more, Mrs Drabdump. Did you ever see anything—say when Miss Dymond came to your house—to make you suspect anything between Mr Constant and the prisoner's sweetheart?'

'She did meet him once when Mr Mortlake was out.' (*Sensation.*)

'Where did she meet him?'

'In the passage. He was going out when she knocked and he opened the door.' (*Amusement.*)

'You didn't hear what they said?'

'I ain't a eavesdropper. They spoke friendly and went away together.'

Mr George Grodman was called and repeated his evidence at the inquest. Cross-examined, he testified to the warm friendship between Mr Constant and the prisoner. He knew very little about Miss Dymond, having scarcely seen her. Prisoner had never spoken to him much about her. He should not think she was much in prisoner's thoughts. Naturally the prisoner had been depressed by the death of his friend. Besides, he was overworked. Witness thought highly of Mortlake's character. It was incredible that Constant had had improper relations of any kind with his friend's promised wife. Grodman's evidence made a very favourable impression on the jury; the prisoner looked his gratitude; and the prosecution felt sorry it had been necessary to call this witness.

Inspector Howlett and Sergeant Runnymede had also to repeat their evidence. Dr Robinson, police-surgeon, likewise re-tendered his evidence as to the nature of the wound, and the approximate hour of death. But this time he was much more severely examined. He would not bind himself down to state the time within an hour or two. He thought life had been extinct two or three hours when he arrived, so that the deed had been committed between seven and eight. Under gentle pressure from the prosecuting counsel, he admitted that it might possibly have been between six and seven. Cross-examined, he reiterated his impression in favour of the later hour.

Supplementary evidence from medical experts proved as dubious and uncertain as if the court had confined itself to the original witness. It seemed to be generally agreed that the data for determining the time of death of anybody were too complex and variable to admit of very precise inference; rigor mortis and other symptoms setting in within very wide limits and differing largely in different persons. All agreed that death from such a cut must have been practically instantaneous, and the theory of suicide was rejected by all. As a whole the medical evidence tended to fix the time of death, with a high degree of probability, between the hours of six and half-past eight. The efforts of the prosecution were bent upon throwing back the time of death to as early as possible after about half-past five. The defence spent all its strength upon pinning the experts to the conclusion that death could not have been earlier than seven. Evidently the prosecution was going to fight hard for the hypothesis that Mortlake had committed the crime in the interval between the first and second trains for Liverpool; while the defence was concentrating itself on an alibi, showing that the prisoner had travelled by the second train which left Euston Station at a quarter past seven, so that there could have been no possible time for the passage between Bow and Euston. It was an exciting struggle. As yet the contending forces seemed equally matched. The evidence had gone as much for as against the prisoner. But everybody knew that worse lay behind.

'Call Edward Wimp.'

The story Edward Wimp had to tell began tamely enough with thrice-threshed-out facts. But at last the new facts came.

'In consequence of suspicions that had formed in your mind you took up your quarters, disguised, in the late Mr Constant's rooms?'

'I did; at the commencement of the year. My suspicions had gradually gathered against the occupants of No. 11, Glover Street, and I resolved to quash or confirm these suspicions once for all.'

'Will you tell the jury what followed?'

'Whenever the prisoner was away for the night I searched his room. I found the key of Mr Constant's bedroom buried deeply in the side of prisoner's leather sofa. I found what I imagine to be the letter he received on December 3rd, in the pages of a "Bradshaw" lying under the same sofa. There were two razors about.'

Mr Spigot, Q.C., said: 'The key has already been identified by Mrs Drabdump. The letter I now propose to read.'

It was undated, and ran as follows:

'Dear Tom—This is to bid you farewell. It is the best for us all. I am going a long way, dearest. Do not seek to find me, for it will be useless. Think of me as one swallowed up by the waters, and be assured that it is only to spare you shame and humiliation in the future that I tear myself from you and all the sweetness of life. Darling, there is no other way. I feel you could never marry me now. I have felt it for months. Dear Tom, you will understand what I mean. We must look facts in the face. I hope you will always be friends with Mr Constant. Good-bye, dear. God bless you! May you always be happy, and find a worthier wife than I. Perhaps when you are great, and rich, and famous, as you deserve, you will sometimes think not unkindly of one who, however faulty and unworthy of you, will at least love you till the end.

   'Yours, till death,
      '*Jessie.*'

By the time this letter was finished numerous old gentlemen, with wigs or without, were observed to be polishing their glasses. Mr Wimp's examination was resumed.

'After making these discoveries what did you do?'

'I made inquiries about Miss Dymond, and found Mr Constant had visited her once or twice in the evening. I imagined there would be some traces of a pecuniary connection. I was allowed by the family to inspect Mr Constant's cheque-book, and found a paid cheque made out for £25 in the name of Miss Dymond. By inquiry at the Bank, I found it had been cashed on November 12th of last year. I then applied for a warrant against the prisoner.'

Cross-examined: 'Do you suggest that the prisoner opened Mr Constant's bedroom with the key you found?'

'Certainly.'

BROWN-HARLAND, Q.C. (*sarcastically*): 'And locked the door from within with it on leaving?'

'Certainly.'

'Will you have the goodness to explain how the trick was done?'

'It wasn't done. (*Laughter.*) The prisoner probably locked the door from the outside. Those who broke it open naturally imagined it had been locked from the inside when they found the key inside. The key would, on this theory, be on the floor as the outside locking could not have been effected if it had been in the lock. The first persons to enter the room would naturally believe it had been thrown down in the bursting of the door. Or it might have been left sticking very loosely inside the lock so as not to interfere with the turning of the outside key in which case it would also probably have been thrown to the ground.'

'Indeed. Very ingenious. And can you also explain how the prisoner could have bolted the door within from the outside?'

'I can. (*Renewed sensation.*) There is only one way in which it was possible—and that was, of course, a mere conjurer's illusion. To cause a locked door to appear bolted in addition, it would only be necessary for the person on the inside of the door to wrest the staple containing the bolt from the woodwork. The bolt in Mr Constant's bedroom worked perpendicularly. When the staple was torn off, it would simply remain at rest on the pin of the bolt instead of supporting it or keeping it fixed. A person bursting open the door and finding the staple resting on the pin and torn away from the lintel of the door would, of course, imagine he had torn it away, never dreaming the wresting off had been done beforehand.' (*Applause in court, which was instantly checked by the ushers.*) The counsel for the defence felt he had been entrapped in attempting to be sarcastic with the redoubtable detective. Grodman seemed green with envy. It was the one thing he had not thought of.

Mrs Drabdump, Grodman, Inspector Howlett, and Sergeant Runnymede were recalled and re-examined by the embarrassed Sir Charles Brown-Harland as to the exact condition of the lock and the bolt and the position of the key. It turned out as Wimp had suggested; so prepossessed were the witnesses with the conviction that the door was locked and bolted from the inside when it was burst open that they were a little hazy about the exact details. The damage had been repaired, so that it was all a question of precise past observation. The inspector and the sergeant testified that the key was in the lock when they saw it, though both the mortice and the bolt were broken. They were not prepared to say that Wimp's theory was impossible; they would even admit it was quite possible that the staple of the bolt had been torn off beforehand. Mrs Drabdump could give no clear account of such petty facts in view of her immediate engrossing interest in the horrible sight of the corpse. Grodman alone was posi- tive that the key was in the door when he burst it open. No, he did not remember picking it up from the floor and putting it in. And he was certain that the staple of the bolt was *not* broken, from the resistance he experienced in trying to shake the upper panels of the door.

By the Prosecution: 'Don't you think, from the compara- tive ease with which the door yielded to your onslaught, that it is highly probable that the pin of the bolt was not in a firmly fixed staple, but in one already detached from the woodwork of the lintel?'

'The door did not yield so easily.'

'But you must be a Hercules.'

'Not quite; the bolt was old, and the woodwork crum- bling; the lock was new and shoddy. But I have always been a strong man.'

'Very well, Mr Grodman. I hope you will never appear at the music-halls.' (*Laughter*.)

Jessie Dymond's landlady was the next witness for the prosecution. She corroborated Wimp's statements as to Constant's occasional visits, and narrated how the girl had been enlisted by the dead philanthropist as a collaborator in some of his enterprises. But the most telling portion of her evidence was the story of how, late at night, on December 3rd, the prisoner called upon her and inquired wildly about the whereabouts of his sweetheart. He said he had just received a mysterious letter from Miss Dymond saying she was gone. She (the landlady) replied that she could have told him that weeks ago, as her ungrateful lodger was gone now some three weeks without leaving a hint behind her. In answer to his most ungentlemanly raging and raving, she told him it served him right, as he should have looked after her better, and not kept away for so long. She reminded him that there were as good fish in the sea as ever came out, and a girl of Jessie's attractions need not pine away (as she had seemed to be pining away) for lack of appreciation. He then called her a liar and left her, and she hoped never to see his face again, though she was not surprised to see it in the dock.

Mr Fitzjames Montgomery, a bank clerk, remembered cashing the check produced. He particularly remembered it, because he paid the money to a very pretty girl. She took the entire amount in gold. At this point the case was adjourned.

Denzil Cantercot was the first witness called for the prosecution on the resumption of the trial. Pressed as to whether he had not told Mr Wimp that he had overheard the prisoner denouncing Mr Constant, he could not say. He had not actually heard the prisoner's denunciations; he might have given Mr Wimp a false impression, but then Mr Wimp was so prosaically literal. (*Laughter*.) Mr Crowl had told him something of the kind. Cross-examined, he said

Jessie Dymond was a rare spirit and she always reminded him of Joan of Arc.

Mr Crowl, being called, was extremely agitated. He refused to take the oath, and informed the court that the Bible was a Fad. He could not swear by anything so self-contradictory. He would affirm. He could not deny—though he looked like wishing to—that the prisoner had at first been rather mistrustful of Mr Constant, but he was certain that the feeling had quickly worn off. Yes, he was a great friend of the prisoner, but he didn't see why that should invalidate his testimony, especially as he had not taken an oath. Certainly the prisoner seemed rather depressed when he saw him on Bank Holiday, but it was overwork on behalf of the people and for the demolition of the Fads.

Several other familiars of the prisoner gave more or less reluctant testimony as to his sometime prejudice against the amateur rival labour leader. His expressions of dislike had been strong and bitter. The prosecution also produced a poster announcing that the prisoner would preside at a great meeting of clerks on December 4th. He had not turned up at this meeting nor sent any explanation. Finally, there was the evidence of the detectives who originally arrested him at Liverpool Docks in view of his suspicious demeanour. This completed the case for the prosecution.

Sir Charles Brown-Harland, Q.C., rose with a swagger and a rustle of his silk gown, and proceeded to set forth the theory of the defence. He said he did not purpose to call any witnesses. The hypothesis of the prosecution was so inherently childish and inconsequential, and so dependent upon a bundle of interdependent probabilities that it crumbled away at the merest touch. The prisoner's character was of unblemished integrity, his last public appearance had been made on the same platform with Mr Gladstone, and his honesty and highmindedness had been vouched for by statesmen of the highest standing. His movements could be accounted for from hour to hour—and those with which the prosecution credited him rested on no tangible evidence whatever. He was also credited with superhuman ingenuity and diabolical cunning of which he had shown no previous symptom. Hypothesis was piled on hypothesis, as in the old Oriental legend, where the world rested on the elephant and the elephant on the tortoise. It might be worth while, however, to point out that it was at least quite likely that the death of Mr Constant had not taken place before seven, and as the prisoner left Euston Station at 7:15 a.m. for Liverpool, he could certainly not have got there from Bow in the time; also that it was hardly possible for the prisoner, who could prove being at Euston Station at 5:25 a.m., to travel backwards and forwards to Glover Street and commit the crime all within less than two hours. 'The real facts,' said Sir Charles impressively, 'are most simple. The prisoner, partly from pressure of work, partly (he had no wish to conceal) from worldly ambition, had begun to neglect Miss Dymond, to whom he was engaged to be married. The man was but human, and his head was a little turned by his growing importance. Nevertheless, at heart he was still deeply attached to Miss Dymond. She, however, appears to have jumped to the conclusion that he had ceased to love her, that she was unworthy of him, unfitted by education to take her place side by side with him in the new spheres to which he was mounting—that, in short, she was a drag on his career. Being, by all accounts, a girl of remarkable force of character, she resolved to cut the Gordian knot by leaving London, and, fearing lest her affianced husband's conscientiousness should induce him to sacrifice himself to her; dreading also, perhaps, her own weakness, she made the parting absolute, and the place of her refuge a mystery. A theory has been suggested which drags an honoured name in the mire—a theory so superfluous that I shall only allude to it. That Arthur Constant could have seduced, or had any improper relations with, his friend's betrothed is a hypothesis to which the lives of both give the lie. Before leaving London—or England—Miss Dymond wrote to her aunt in Devonport—her only living relative in this country—asking her as a great favour to forward an addressed letter to the prisoner, a fortnight after receipt. The aunt obeyed implicitly. This was the letter which fell like a thunderbolt on the prisoner on the night of December 3rd. All his old love returned—he was full of self-reproach and pity for the poor girl. The letter read ominously. Perhaps she was going to put an end to herself. His first thought was to rush up to his friend, Constant, to seek his advice. Perhaps Constant knew something of the affair. The prisoner knew the two were in not infrequent communication. It is possible—my lord and gentlemen of the jury, I do not wish to follow the methods of the prosecution and confuse theory with fact, so I say it is possible—that Mr Constant had supplied her with the £25 to leave the country. He was like a brother to her, perhaps even acted imprudently in calling upon her, though neither dreamed of evil. It is possible that he may have encouraged her in her abnegation and in her altruistic aspirations, perhaps even without knowing their exact drift, for does he not speak in his very last letter of the fine female characters he was meeting, and the influence for good he had over individual human souls? Still, this we can now never know, unless the dead speak or the absent return. It is also not impossible that Miss Dymond was entrusted with the £25 for charitable purposes. But to come back to certainties. The prisoner consulted Mr Constant about the letter. He then ran to Miss Dymond's lodgings in Stepney Green, knowing beforehand his trouble would be futile. The letter bore the postmark of Devonport. He knew the girl had an aunt there; possibly she might have gone to her. He could not telegraph, for he was ignorant of the address. He consulted his 'Bradshaw', and resolved to leave by the 5:30 a.m. from Paddington, and told his landlady so. He left the letter in the 'Bradshaw,' which ultimately got thrust among a pile of papers under the sofa, so that he had to get another. He was careless and disorderly, and the key found by Mr Wimp in his sofa must have lain there for some years, having been lost there in the days when he occupied the bedroom afterwards rented by Mr Constant. Afraid to miss his train, he did not undress on that distressful night. Meantime the thought occurred to him that Jessie was too clever a girl to leave so easy a trail, and he jumped to the conclusion that she would be going to her married brother in America, and had gone to Devonport merely to bid her aunt farewell. He determined therefore to get to Liverpool, without wasting time at Devonport, to institute inquiries. Not suspecting the delay in the transit of the letter, he thought he might yet stop her, even at the landing-stage or on the tender. Unfortunately his cab went slowly in the fog, he missed the first train, and wandered about brooding disconsolately in the mist till the second. At Liverpool his suspicious, excited demeanour procured his momentary arrest. Since then the thought of the lost girl has haunted and broken him. That is the whole, the plain, and the sufficing story.'

The effective witnesses for the defence were, indeed, few. It is so hard to prove a negative. There was Jessie's aunt, who bore out the statement of the counsel for the defence. There were the porters who saw him leave Euston by the 7:15 train for Liverpool, and arrive just too late for the 5:15; there was the cabman (2138), who drove him to Euston just in time, he (witness) thought, to catch the 5:15 a.m. Under cross-examination, the cabman got a little confused; he was asked whether, if he really picked up the prisoner at Bow Railway Station at about 4:30, he ought not to have caught the first train at Euston. He said the fog made him drive rather slowly, but admitted the mist was transparent enough to warrant full speed. He also admitted being a strong trade unionist, Spigot, Q.C., artfully extorting the admission as if it were of the utmost significance. Finally, there were numerous witnesses—of all sorts and conditions—to the prisoner's high character, as well as to Arthur Constant's blameless and moral life.

In his closing speech on the third day of the trial, Sir Charles pointed out with great exhaustiveness and cogency the flimsiness of the case for the prosecution, the number of hypotheses it involved, and their mutual interdependence. Mrs Drabdump was a witness whose evidence must be accepted with extreme caution. The jury must remember that she was unable to dissociate her observations from her inferences, and thought that the prisoner and Mr Constant were quarrelling merely because they were agitated. He dissected her evidence, and showed that it entirely bore out the story of the defence. He asked the jury to bear in mind that no positive evidence (whether of cabmen or others) had been given of the various and complicated movements attributed to the prisoner on the morning of December 4th, between the hours of 5:25 and 7:15 a.m., and that the most important witness on the theory of the prosecution—he meant, of course, Miss Dymond—had not been produced. Even if she were dead, and her body were found, no countenance would be given to the theory of the prosecution, for the mere conviction that her lover had deserted her would be a sufficient explanation of her suicide. Beyond the ambiguous letter, no tittle of evidence of her dishonour—on which the bulk of the case against the prisoner rested—had been adduced. As for the motive of political jealousy that had been a mere passing cloud. The two men had become fast friends. As to the circumstances of the alleged crime, the medical evidence was on the whole in favour of the time of death being late; and the prisoner had left London at a quarter past seven. The drugging theory was absurd, and as for the too-clever bolt and lock theories, Mr Grodman, a trained scientific observer, had pooh-poohed them. He would solemnly exhort the jury to remember that if they condemned the prisoner they would not only send an innocent man to an ignominious death on the flimsiest circumstantial evidence, but they would deprive the working-men of this country of one of their truest friends and their ablest leader.

The conclusion of Sir Charles' vigorous speech was greeted with irrepressible applause.

Mr Spigot, Q.C., in closing the case for the prosecution, asked the jury to return a verdict against the prisoner for as malicious and premeditated a crime as ever disgraced the annals of any civilized country. His cleverness and education had only been utilized for the devil's ends, while his reputation had been used as a cloak. Everything pointed strongly to the prisoner's guilt. On receiving Miss Dymond's letter announcing her shame, and (probably) her intention to commit suicide, he had hastened upstairs to denounce Constant. He had then rushed to the girl's lodgings, and, finding his worst fears confirmed, planned at once his diabolically ingenious scheme of revenge. He told his landlady he was going to Devonport, so that if he bungled, the police would be put temporarily off his track. His real destination was Liverpool, for he intended to leave the country. Lest, however, his plan should break down here, too, he arranged an ingenious alibi by being driven to Euston for the 5:15 train to Liverpool. The cabman would not know he did not intend to go by it, but meant to return to 11 Glover Street, there to perpetrate this foul crime, interruption to which he had possibly barred by drugging his landlady. His presence at Liverpool (whither he really went by the second train) would corroborate the cabman's story. That night he had not undressed nor gone to bed; he had plotted out his devilish scheme till it was perfect; the fog came as an unexpected ally to cover his movements. Jealousy, outraged affection, the desire for revenge, the lust for political power—these were human. They might pity the criminal, they could not find him innocent of the crime.

Mr Justice Crogie, summing up, began dead against the prisoner. Reviewing the evidence, he pointed out that plausible hypotheses neatly dovetailed did not necessarily weaken one another, the fitting so well together of the whole rather making for the truth of the parts. Besides, the case for the prosecution was as far from being all hypothesis as the case for the defence was from excluding hypothesis. The key, the letter, the reluctance to produce the letter, the heated interview with Constant, the misstatement about the prisoner's destination, the flight to Liverpool, the false tale about searching for a 'him', the denunciations of Constant, all these were facts. On the other hand, there were various lacunae and hypotheses in the case for the defence. Even conceding the somewhat dubious alibi afforded by the prisoner's presence at Euston at 5:25 a.m., there was no attempt to account for his movements between that and 7:15 a.m. It was as possible that he returned to Bow as that he lingered about Euston. There was nothing in the medical evidence to make his guilt impossible. Nor was there anything inherently impossible in Constant's yielding to the sudden temptation of a beautiful girl, nor in a working-girl deeming herself deserted, temporarily succumbing to the fascinations of a gentleman and regretting it bitterly afterward. What had become of the girl was a mystery. Hers might have been one of those nameless corpses which the tide swirls up on slimy river banks. The jury must remember, too, that the relation might not have actually passed into dishonour, it might have been just grave enough to smite the girl's conscience, and to induce her to behave as she had done. It was enough that her letter should have excited the jealousy of the prisoner. There was one other point which he would like to impress on the jury, and which the counsel for the prosecution had not sufficiently insisted upon. This was that the prisoner's guiltiness was the only plausible solution that had ever been advanced of the Bow Mystery. The medical evidence agreed that Mr Constant did not die by his own hand. Someone must therefore have murdered him. The number of people who could have had any possible reason or opportunity to murder him was extremely small. The prisoner had both reason and opportunity. By what logicians called the method of exclusion, suspicion would attach to him on even slight evidence. The actual evidence was strong and plausible, and now that Mr Wimp's ingenious theory had enabled them to understand how the door could have been apparently locked and bolted from within, the last difficulty and the last argument for suicide had been removed. The prisoner's guilt was as clear as circumstantial evidence could make it. If they let him go free, the Bow Mystery might henceforward be placed among the archives of unavenged assassinations. Having thus well-nigh hung the prisoner, the judge wound up by insisting on the high probability of the story for the defence, though that, too, was dependent in important details upon the prisoner's mere private statements to his counsel. The jury, being by this time sufficiently muddled by his impartiality, were dismissed, with the exhortation to allow due weight to every fact and probability in determining their righteous verdict.

The minutes ran into hours, but the jury did not return. The shadows of night fell across the reeking, fevered court before they announced their verdict—

'Guilty.'

The judge put on his black cap.

The great reception arranged outside was a fiasco; the evening banquet was indefinitely postponed. Wimp had won; Grodman felt like a whipped cur.

CHAPTER XI

'So you were right,' Denzil could not help saying as he greeted Grodman a week afterwards. 'I shall *not* live to tell the story of how you discovered the Bow murderer.'

'Sit down,' growled Grodman; 'perhaps you will after all.' There was a dangerous gleam in his eyes. Denzil was sorry he had spoken.

'I sent for you,' Grodman said, 'to tell you that on the night Wimp arrested Mortlake I had made preparations for your arrest.'

Denzil gasped, 'What for?'

'My dear Denzil, there is a little law in this country invented for the confusion of the poetic. The greatest exponent of the Beautiful is only allowed the same number of wives as the greengrocer. I do not blame you for not being satisfied with Jane—she is a good servant but a bad mistress—but it was cruel to Kitty not to inform her that Jane had a prior right in you, and unjust to Jane not to let her know of the contract with Kitty.'

'They both know it now well enough, curse 'em,' said the poet.

'Yes; your secrets are like your situations—you can't keep them long. My poor poet, I pity you—betwixt the devil and the deep sea.'

'They're a pair of harpies, each holding over me the Damocles sword of an arrest for bigamy. Neither loves me.'

'I should think they would come in very useful to you. You plant one in my house to tell my secrets to Wimp, and you plant one in Wimp's house to tell Wimp's secrets to me, I suppose. Out with some, then.'

'Upon my honour you wrong me. Jane brought *me* here, not I Jane. As for Kitty, I never had such a shock in my life as at finding her installed in Wimp's house.'

'She thought it safer to have the law handy for your arrest. Besides, she probably desired to occupy a parallel position to Jane's. She must do something for a living; *you* wouldn't do anything for hers. And so you couldn't go anywhere without meeting a wife! Ha! ha! ha! Serve you right, my polygamous poet.'

'But why should *you* arrest me?'

'Revenge, Denzil. I have been the best friend you ever had in this cold, prosaic world. You have eaten my bread, drunk my claret, written my book, smoked my cigars, and pocketed my money. And yet, when you have an important piece of information bearing on a mystery about which I am thinking day and night, you calmly go and sell it to Wimp.'

'I did-didn't,' stammered Denzil.

'Liar! Do you think Kitty has any secrets from me? As soon as I discovered your two marriages I determined to have you arrested for—your treachery. But when I found you had, as I thought, put Wimp on the wrong scent, when I felt sure that by arresting Mortlake he was going to make a greater ass of himself than even nature had been able to do, then I forgave you. I let you walk about the earth—and drink—freely. Now it is Wimp who crows—everybody pats him on the back—they call him the mystery man of the Scotland Yard tribe. Poor Tom Mortlake will be hanged, and all through your telling Wimp about Jessie Dymond!'

'It was you yourself,' said Denzil sullenly. 'Everybody was giving it up. But you said 'Let us find out all that Arthur Constant did in the last few months of his life.' Wimp couldn't miss stumbling on Jessie sooner or later. I'd have throttled Constant, if I had known he'd touched her,' he wound up with irrelevant indignation.

Grodman winced at the idea that he himself had worked *ad majorem gloriam* of Wimp. And yet, had not Mrs Wimp let out as much at the Christmas dinner?

'What's past is past,' he said gruffly. 'But if Tom Mortlake hangs, you go to Portland.'

'How can I help Tom hanging?'

'Help the agitation as much as you can. Write letters under all sorts of names to all the papers. Get everybody you know to sign the great petition. Find out where Jessie Dymond is—the girl who holds the proof of Tom Mortlake's innocence.'

'You really believe him innocent?'

'Don't be satirical, Denzil. Haven't I taken the chair at all the meetings? Am I not the most copious correspondent of the Press?'

'I thought it was only to spite Wimp.'

'Rubbish. It's to save poor Tom. He no more murdered Arthur Constant than—you did!' He laughed an unpleasant laugh.

Denzil bade him farewell, frigid with fear.

Grodman was up to his ears in letters and telegrams. Somehow he had become the leader of the rescue party—suggestions, subscriptions came from all sides. The suggestions were burnt, the subscriptions acknowledged in the papers and used for hunting up the missing girl. Lucy Brent headed the list with a hundred pounds. It was a fine testimony to her faith in her dead lover's honour.

The release of the Jury had unloosed 'The Greater Jury', which always now sits upon the smaller. Every means was taken to nullify the value of the 'palladium of British liberty'. The foreman and the jurors were interviewed, the judge was judged, and by those who were no judges. The Home Secretary (who had done nothing beyond accepting office under the Crown) was vituperated, and sundry provincial persons wrote confidentially to the Queen. Arthur Constant's backsliding cheered many by convincing them that others were as bad as themselves; and well-to-do tradesmen saw in Mortlake's wickedness the pernicious effects of socialism. A dozen new theories were afloat. Constant had committed suicide by Esoteric Buddhism, as witness his devotion to Mme Blavatsky, or he had been murdered by his Mahatma, or victimized by Hypnotism, Mesmerism, Somnambulism, and other weird abstractions. Grodman's great point was—Jessie Dymond must be produced, dead or alive. The electric current scoured the civilized world in search of her. What wonder if the shrewder sort divined that the indomitable detective had fixed his last hope on the girl's guilt? If Jessie had wrongs why should she not have avenged them herself? Did she not always remind the poet of Joan of Arc?

Another week passed; the shadow of the gallows crept over the days; on, on, remorselessly drawing nearer, as the last ray of hope sank below the horizon. The Home Secretary remained inflexible; the great petitions discharged their signatures at him in vain. He was a Conservative, sternly conscientious; and the mere insinuation that his obstinacy was due to the politics of the condemned only hardened him against the temptation of a cheap reputation for magnanimity. He would not even grant a respite, to increase the chances of the discovery of Jessie Dymond. In the last of the three weeks there was a final monster meeting of protest. Grodman again took the chair, and several distinguished faddists were present, as well as numerous respectable members of society. The Home Secretary acknowledged the receipt of their resolutions. The Trade Unions were divided in their allegiance; some whispered of faith and hope, others of financial defalcations. The former essayed to organize a procession and an indignation meeting on the Sunday preceding the Tuesday fixed for the execution, but it fell through on a rumour of confession. The Monday papers contained a last masterly letter from Grodman exposing the weakness of the evidence, but they knew nothing of a confession. The prisoner was mute and disdainful, professing little regard for a life empty of love and burdened with self-reproach. He refused to see clergymen. He was accorded an interview with Miss Brent in the presence of a gaoler, and solemnly asseverated his respect for her dead lover's memory. Monday buzzed with rumours; the evening papers chronicled them hour by hour. A poignant anxiety was abroad.

The girl would be found. Some miracle would happen. A reprieve would arrive. The sentence would be commuted. But the short day darkened into night even as Mortlake's short day was darkening. And the shadow of the gallows crept on and on and seemed to mingle with the twilight.

Crowl stood at the door of his shop, unable to work. His big grey eyes were heavy with unshed tears. The dingy wintry road seemed one vast cemetery; the street lamps twinkled like corpse-lights. The confused sounds of the street-life reached his ear as from another world. He did not see the people who flitted to and fro amid the gathering shadows of the cold, dreary night. One ghastly vision flashed and faded and flashed upon the background of the duskiness.

Denzil stood beside him, smoking in silence. A cold fear was at his heart. That terrible Grodman! As the hangman's cord was tightening round Mortlake, he felt the convict's chains tightening round himself. And yet there was one gleam of hope, feeble as the yellow flicker of the gas-lamp across the way. Grodman had obtained an interview with the condemned late that afternoon, and the parting had been painful, but the evening paper, that in its turn had obtained an interview with the ex-detective, announced on its placard

'GRODMAN STILL CONFIDENT'

and the thousands who yet pinned their faith on this extraordinary man refused to extinguish the last sparks of hope. Denzil had bought the paper and scanned it eagerly, but there was nothing save the vague assurance that the indefatigable Grodman was still almost pathetically expectant of the miracle. Denzil did not share the expectation; he meditated flight.

'Peter,' he said at last, 'I'm afraid it's all over.'

Crowl nodded, heart-broken. 'All over!' he repeated, 'and to think that he dies—and it is—all over!'

He looked despairingly at the blank winter sky, where leaden clouds shut out the stars. 'Poor, poor young fellow! Tonight alive and thinking. Tomorrow night a clod, with no more sense or motion than a bit of leather! No compensation nowhere for being cut off innocent in the pride of youth and strength! A man who has always preached the Useful day and night, and toiled and suffered for his fellows. Where's the justice of it, where's the justice of it?' he demanded fiercely. Again his wet eyes wandered upward toward heaven, that heaven away from which the soul of a dead saint at the Antipodes was speeding into infinite space.

'Well, where was the justice for Arthur Constant if he, too, was innocent?' said Denzil. 'Really, Peter, I don't see why you should take it for granted that Tom is so dreadfully injured. Your horny-handed labour leaders are, after all, men of no aesthetic refinement, with no sense of the Beautiful; you cannot expect them to be exempt from the coarser forms of crime. Humanity must look to for other leaders—to the seers and the poets!'

'Cantercot, if you say Tom's guilty I'll knock you down.' The little cobbler turned upon his tall friend like a roused lion. Then he added, 'I beg your pardon, Cantercot, I don't mean that. After all, I've no grounds. The judge is an honest man, and with gifts I can't lay claim to. But I believe in Tom with all my heart. And if Tom is guilty I believe in the Cause of the People with all my heart all the same. The Fads are doomed to death, they may be reprieved, but they must die at last.'

He drew a deep sigh, and looked along the dreary road. It was quite dark now, but by the light of the lamps and the gas in the shop windows the dull, monotonous road lay revealed in all its sordid, familiar outlines; with its long stretches of chill pavement, its unlovely architecture, and its endless stream of prosaic pedestrians.

A sudden consciousness of the futility of his existence pierced the little cobbler like an icy wind. He saw his own life, and a hundred million lives like his, swelling and breaking like bubbles on a dark ocean, unheeded, uncared for.

A news-boy passed along, clamouring 'The Bow murderer, preparaytions for the hexecution!'

A terrible shudder shook the cobbler's frame. His eyes ranged sightlessly after the boy; the merciful tears filled them at last.

'The Cause of the People,' he murmured, brokenly, 'I believe in the Cause of the People. There is nothing else.'

'Peter, come in to tea, you'll catch cold,' said Mrs Crowl.

Denzil went in to tea and Peter followed.

Meantime, round the house of the Home Secretary, who was in town, an ever-augmenting crowd was gathered, eager to catch the first whisper of a reprieve.

The house was guarded by a cordon of police, for there was no inconsiderable danger of a popular riot. At times a section of the crowd groaned and hooted. Once a volley of stones was discharged at the windows. The news-boys were busy vending their special editions, and the reporters struggled through the crowd, clutching descriptive pencils, and ready to rush off to telegraph offices should anything 'extra special' occur. Telegraph boys were coming up every now and again with threats, messages, petitions and exhortations from all parts of the country to the unfortunate Home Secretary, who was striving to keep his aching head cool as he went through the voluminous evidence for the last time and pondered over the more important letters which 'The Greater Jury' had contributed to the obscuration of the problem. Grodman's letter in that morning's paper shook him most; under his scientific analysis the circumstantial chain seemed forged of painted cardboard. Then the poor man read the judge's summing up, and the chain became tempered steel. The noise of the crowd outside broke upon his ear in his study like the roar of a distant ocean. The more the rabble hooted him, the more he essayed to hold scrupulously the scales of life and death. And the crowd grew and grew, as men came away from their work. There were many that loved the man who lay in the jaws of death, and a spirit of mad revolt surged in their breasts. And the sky was grey, and the bleak night deepened and the shadow of the gallows crept on.

Suddenly a strange inarticulate murmur spread through the crowd, a vague whisper of no one knew what. Something had happened. Somebody was coming. A second later and one of the outskirts of the throng was agitated, and a convulsive cheer went up from it, and was taken up infectiously all along the street. The crowd parted—a hansom dashed through the centre. 'Grodman! Grodman!' shouted those who recognized the occupant. 'Grodman! Hurrah!' Grodman was outwardly calm and pale, but his eyes glittered; he waved his hand encouragingly as the hansom dashed up to the door, cleaving the turbulent crowd as a canoe cleaves the waters. Grodman sprang out, the constables at the portal made way for him respectfully. He knocked imperatively, the door was opened cautiously; a boy rushed up and delivered a telegram; Grodman forced his way in, gave his name, and insisted on seeing the Home Secretary on a matter of life and death. Those near the door heard his words and cheered, and the crowd divined the good omen, and the air throbbed with cannonades of joyous sound. The cheers rang in Grodman's ears as the door slammed behind him. The reporters struggled to the front. An excited knot of working men pressed round the arrested hansom, they took the horse out. A dozen enthusiasts struggled for the honour of placing themselves between the shafts. And the crowd awaited Grodman.

CHAPTER XII

GRODMAN was ushered into the conscientious Minister's study. The doughty chief of the agitation was, perhaps, the one man who could not be denied. As he entered, the Home Secretary's face seemed lit up with relief. At a sign from his master, the amanuensis who had brought in the last telegram took it back with him into the outer room where he worked. Needless to say not a tithe of the Minister's correspondence ever came under his own eyes.

'You have a valid reason for troubling me, I suppose, Mr Grodman?' said the Home Secretary, almost cheerfully. 'Of course it is about Mortlake?'

'It is; and I have the best of all reasons.'

'Take a seat. Proceed.'

'Pray do not consider me impertinent, but have you ever given any attention to the science of evidence?'

'How do you mean?' asked the Home Secretary, rather puzzled, adding, with a melancholy smile, 'I have had to lately. Of course, I've never been a criminal lawyer, like some of my predecessors. But I should hardly speak of it as a science; I look upon it as a question of common-sense.'

'Pardon me, sir. It is the most subtle and difficult of all the sciences. It is, indeed, rather the science of the sciences. What is the whole of Inductive Logic, as laid down, say, by Bacon and Mill, but an attempt to appraise the value of evidence, the said evidence being the trails left by the Creator, so to speak? The Creator has—I say it in all reverence—drawn a myriad red herrings across the track, but the true scientist refuses to be baffled by superficial appearances in detecting the secrets of Nature. The vulgar herd catches at the gross apparent fact, but the man of insight knows that what lies on the surface does lie.'

'Very interesting, Mr Grodman, but really—'

'Bear with me, sir. The science of evidence being thus so extremely subtle, and demanding the most acute and trained observation of facts, the most comprehensive understanding of human psychology, is naturally given over to professors who have not the remotest idea that "things are not what they seem" and that everything is other than it appears; to professors, most of whom by their year-long devotion to the shop-counter or the desk have acquired an intimate acquaintance with all the infinite shades and complexities of things and human nature. When twelve of these professors are put in a box, it is called a jury. When one of these professors is put in a box by himself, he is called a witness. The retailing of evidence—the observation of the facts—is given over to people who go through their lives without eyes; the apprecia- tion of evidence—the judging of these facts—is surrendered to people who may possibly be adepts in weighing out pounds of sugar. Apart from their sheer inability to fulfil either func- tion—to observe, or to judge—their observation and their judgment alike are vitiated by all sorts of irrelevant prejudices.'

'You are attacking trial by jury.'

'Not necessarily. I am prepared to accept that scientifically, on the ground that, as there are, as a rule, only two alterna- tives, the balance of probability is slightly in favour of the true decision being come to. Then, in cases where experts like myself have got up the evidence, the jury can be made to see through trained eyes.'

The Home Secretary tapped impatiently with his foot.

'I can't listen to abstract theorizing,' he said. 'Have you any fresh concrete evidence?'

'Sir, everything depends on our getting down to the root of the matter. What percentage of average evidence should you think is thorough, plain, simple, unvarnished fact, "the truth, the whole truth, and nothing but the truth"?'

'Fifty?' said the Minister, humouring him a little.

'Not five. I say nothing of lapses of memory, of inborn defects of observational power—though the suspiciously precise recollection of dates and events possessed by ordinary witnesses in important trials taking place years after the occurrences involved is one of the most amazing things in the curiosities of modern jurisprudence. I defy you, sir, to tell me what you had for dinner last Monday, or what exactly you were saying and doing at five o'clock last Tuesday afternoon. Nobody whose life does not run in mechanical grooves can do anything of the sort; unless, of course, the facts have been very impressive. But this by the way. The great obstacle to veracious observation is the element of prepossession in all vision. Has it ever struck you, sir, that we never see anyone more than once, if that? The first time we meet a man we may possibly see him as he is; the second time our vision is coloured and modified by the memory of the first. Do our friends appear to us as they appear to strangers? Do our rooms, our furniture, our pipes strike our eye as they would strike the eye of an outsider, looking on them for the first time? Can a mother see her babe's ugliness, or a lover his mistress's shortcomings, though they stare everybody else in the face? Can we see ourselves as others see us? No; habit, prepossession changes all. The mind is a large factor of every so-called external fact. The eye sees, sometimes, what it wishes to see, more often what it expects to see. You follow me, sir?'

The Home Secretary nodded his head less impatiently. He was beginning to be interested. The hubbub from without broke faintly upon their ears.

'To give you a definite example. Mr Wimp says that when I burst open the door of Mr Constant's room on the morning of December 4th, and saw that the staple of the bolt had been wrested by the pin from the lintel, I jumped at once to the conclusion that I had broken the bolt. Now I admit that this was so, only in things like this you do not seem to *conclude*, you jump so fast that you *see*, or seem to. On the other hand, when you *see* a *standing* ring of fire produced by whirling a burning stick, you do *not* believe in its continuous existence. It is the same when witnessing a legerdemain performance. Seeing is not always believing, despite the proverb; but believing is often seeing. It is not to the point that in that little matter of the door Wimp was as hopelessly and incurably wrong as he has been in everything all along. Though the door was securely bolted, I confess that I should have seen that I had broken the bolt in forcing the door, even if it had been broken beforehand. Never once since December 4th did this possibility occur to me, till Wimp with perverted ingenuity suggested it. If this is the case with a trained observer, one moreover fully conscious of this ineradicable tendency of the human mind, how must it be with an untrained observer?'

'Come to the point, come to the point,' said the Home Secretary, putting out his hand as if it itched to touch the bell on the writing-table.

'Such as,' went on Grodman imperturbably, 'such as— Mrs Drabdump. That worthy person is unable, by repeated violent knocking, to arouse her lodger who yet desires to be aroused; she becomes alarmed, she rushes across to get my assistance; I burst open the door—what do you think the good lady expected to see?'

'Mr Constant murdered, I suppose,' murmured the Home Secretary, wonderingly.

'Exactly. And so she saw it. And what should you think was the condition of Arthur Constant when the door yielded to my violent exertions and flew open?'

'Why, was he not dead?' gasped the Home Secretary, his heart fluttering violently.

'Dead? A young, healthy fellow like that! When the door flew open Arthur Constant was sleeping the sleep of the just. It was a deep, a very deep sleep, of course, else the blows at his door would long since have awakened him. But all the while Mrs Drabdump's fancy was picturing her lodger cold and stark the poor young fellow was lying in bed in a nice warm sleep.'

'You mean to say you found Arthur Constant alive?'

'As you were last night.'

The minister was silent, striving confusedly to take in the situation. Outside the crowd was cheering again. It was probably to pass the time.

'Then, when was he murdered?'

'Immediately afterwards.'

'By whom?'

'Well, that is, if you will pardon me, not a very intelligent question. Science and common-sense are in accord for once. Try the method of exhaustion. It must have been either by Mrs Drabdump or by myself.'

'You mean to say that Mrs Drabdump—!'

'Poor dear Mrs Drabdump, you don't deserve this of your Home Secretary! The idea of that good lady!'

'It was *you!*'

'Calm yourself, my dear Home Secretary. There is nothing to be alarmed at. It was a solitary experiment, and I intend it to remain so.' The noise without grew louder. 'Three cheers for Grodman! Hip, hip, hip, hooray,' fell faintly on their ears.

But the Minister, pallid and deeply moved, touched the bell. The Home Secretary's home secretary appeared. He looked at the great man's agitated face with suppressed surprise.

'Thank you for calling in your amanuensis,' said Grodman. 'I intended to ask you to lend me his services. I suppose he can write shorthand.'

The minister nodded, speechless.

'That is well. I intend this statement to form the basis of an appendix to the twenty-fifth edition—sort of silver wedding—of my book, *Criminals I Have Caught*. Mr Denzil Cantercot, who, by the will I have made today, is appointed my literary executor, will have the task of working it up with literary and dramatic touches after the model of the other chapters of my book. I have every confidence he will be able to do me as much justice, from a literary point of view, as you, sir, no doubt will from a legal. I feel certain he will succeed in catching the style of the other chapters to perfection.'

'Templeton,' whispered the Home Secretary, 'this man may be a lunatic. The effort to solve the Big Bow Mystery may have addled his brain. Still,' he added aloud, 'it will be as well for you to take down his statement in shorthand.'

'Thank you, sir,' said Grodman, heartily. 'Ready, Mr Templeton? Here goes. My career till I left the Scotland Yard Detective Department is known to all the world. Is that too fast for you, Mr Templeton? A little? Well, I'll go slower; but pull me up if I forget to keep the brake on. When I retired, I discovered that I was a bachelor. But it was too late to marry. Time hung on my hands. The preparation of my book, *Criminals I Have Caught*, kept me occupied for some months. When it was published I had nothing more to do but think. I had plenty of money, and it was safely invested; there was no call for speculation. The future was meaningless to me; I regretted I had not elected to die in harness. As idle old men must, I lived in the past. I went over and over again my ancient exploits; I re-read my book. And as I thought and thought, away from the excitement of the actual hunt, and seeing the facts in a truer perspective, so it grew daily clearer to me that criminals were more fools than rogues. Every crime I had traced, however cleverly perpetrated, was from the point of view of penetrability a weak failure. Traces and trails were left on all sides—ragged edges, rough-hewn corners; in short, the job was botched, artistic completeness unattained. To the vulgar, my feats might seem marvellous—the average man is mystified to grasp how you detect the letter 'e' in a simple cryptogram—to myself they were as commonplace as the crimes they unveiled. To me now, with my lifelong study of the science of evidence, it seemed possible to commit not merely one, but a thousand crimes that should be absolutely undiscoverable. And yet criminals would go on sinning, and giving themselves away, in the same old grooves—no originality, no dash, no individual insight, no fresh conception! One would imagine there were an Academy of crime with forty thousand armchairs. And gradually, as I pondered and brooded over the thought, there came upon me the desire to commit a crime that should baffle detection. I could invent hundreds of such crimes, and please myself by imagining them done; but would they really work out in practice? Evidently the sole performer of my experiment must be myself; the subject—whom or what? Accident should determine. I itched to commence with murder—to tackle the stiffest problems first, and I burned to startle and baffle the world—especially the world of which I had ceased to be. Outwardly I was calm, and spoke to the people about me as usual. Inwardly I was on fire with a consuming scientific passion. I sported with my pet theories, and fitted them mentally on everyone I met. Every friend or acquaintance I sat and gossiped with, I was plotting how to murder without leaving a clue. There is not one of my friends or acquaintances I have not done away with in thought. There is no public man—have no fear, my dear Home Secretary—I have not planned to assassinate secretly, mysteriously, unintelligibly, undiscoverably. Ah, how I could give the stock criminals points—with their second-hand motives, their conventional conceptions, their commonplace details, their lack of artistic feeling and restraint.

'The late Arthur Constant came to live nearly opposite me. I cultivated his acquaintance—he was a lovable young fellow, an excellent subject for experiment. I do not know when I have ever taken to a man more. From the moment I first set eyes on him, there was a peculiar sympathy between us. We were drawn to each other. I felt instinctively he would be the man. I loved to hear him speak enthusiastically of the Brotherhood of Man—I, who knew the brotherhood of man was to the ape, the serpent, and the tiger—and he seemed to find a pleasure in stealing a moment's chat with me from his engrossing self-appointed duties. It is a pity humanity should have been robbed of so valuable a life. But it had to be. At a quarter to ten on the night of December 3rd he came to me. Naturally I said nothing about this visit at the inquest or the trial. His object was to consult me mysteriously about some girl. He said he had privately lent her money—which she was to repay at her convenience. What the money was for he did not know, except that it was somehow connected with an act of abnegation in which he had vaguely encouraged her. The girl had since disappeared, and he was in distress about her. He would not tell me who it was—of course now, sir, you know as well as I it was Jessie Dymond—but asked for advice as to how to set about finding her. He mentioned that Mortlake was leaving for Devonport by the first train on the next day. Of old I should have connected these two facts and sought the thread; now, as he spoke, all my thoughts were dyed red. He was suffering perceptibly from toothache, and in answer to my sympathetic inquiries told me it had been allowing him very little sleep. Everything combined to invite the trial of one of my favourite theories. I spoke to him in a fatherly way, and when I had tendered some vague advice about the girl, and made him promise to secure a night's rest (before he faced the arduous tram-men's meeting in the morning) by taking a sleeping-draught, I gave him some sulphonal in a phial. It is a new drug, which produces protracted sleep without disturbing the digestion, and which I use myself. He promised faithfully to take the draught; and I also exhorted him earnestly to bolt and bar and lock himself in so as to stop up every chink or aperture by which the cold air of the winter's night might creep into the room. I remonstrated with him on the careless manner he treated his body, and he laughed in his good-humoured, gentle way, and promised to obey me in all things. And he did. That Mrs Drabdump, failing to rouse him, would cry "Murder!" I took for certain. She is built that way. As even Sir Charles Brown-Harland remarked, she habitually takes her prepossessions for facts, her inferences for observations. She forecasts the future in grey. Most women of Mrs Drabdump's class would have behaved as she did. She happened to be a peculiarly favourable specimen for working on by "suggestion", but I would have undertaken to produce the same effect on almost any woman under similar conditions. The only uncertain link in the chain was: Would Mrs Drabdump rush across to get *me* to break open the door? Women always rush for a man. I was well-nigh the nearest, and certainly the most authoritative man in the street, and I took it for granted she would.'

'But suppose she hadn't?' the Home Secretary could not help asking.

'Then the murder wouldn't have happened, that's all. In due course Arthur Constant would have awoke, or somebody else breaking open the door would have found him sleeping; no harm done, nobody any the wiser. I could hardly sleep myself that night. The thought of the extraordinary crime I was about to commit—a burning curiosity to know whether Wimp would detect the *modus operandi*—the prospect of sharing the feelings of murderers with whom I had been in contact all my life without being in touch with the terrible joys of their inner life—the fear lest I should be too fast asleep to hear Mrs Drabdump's knock—these things agitated me and disturbed my rest. I lay tossing on my bed, planning every detail of poor Constant's end. The hours dragged slowly and wretchedly on toward the misty dawn. I was racked with suspense. Was I to be disappointed after all? At last the welcome sound came—the rat-tat-tat of murder. The echoes of that knock are yet in my ear. 'Come over and kill him!' I put my night-capped head out of the window and told her to wait for me. I dressed hurriedly, took my razor, and went across to 11 Glover Street. As I broke open the door of the bedroom in which Arthur Constant lay sleeping, his head resting on his hands, I cried, 'My God!' as if I saw some awful vision. A mist as of blood swam before Mrs Drabdump's eyes. She cowered back, for an instant (I divined rather than saw the action) she shut off the dreaded sight with her hands. In that instant I had made my cut—precisely, scientifically—made so deep a cut and drew out the weapon so sharply that there was scarce a drop of blood on it; then there came from the throat a jet of blood which Mrs Drabdump, conscious only of the horrid gash, saw but vaguely. I covered up the face quickly with a handkerchief to hide any convulsive distortion. But as the medical evidence (in this detail accurate) testified, death was instantaneous. I pocketed the razor and the empty sulphonal phial. With a woman like Mrs Drabdump to watch me, I could do anything I pleased. I got her to draw my attention to the fact that both the windows were fastened. Some fool, by the by, thought there was a discrepancy in the evidence because the police found only one window fastened, forgetting that, in my innocence, I took care not to fasten the window I had opened to call for aid. Naturally I did not call for aid before a considerable time had elapsed. There was Mrs Drabdump to quiet, and the excuse of making notes—as an old hand. My object was to gain time. I wanted the body to be fairly cold and stiff before being discovered, though there was not much danger here; for, as you saw by the medical evidence, there is no telling the time of death to an hour or two. The frank way in which I said the death was very recent disarmed all suspicion, and even Dr Robinson was unconsciously worked upon, in adjudging the time of death, by the knowledge (query here, Mr Templeton) that it had preceded my advent on the scene.

'Before leaving Mrs Drabdump there is just one point I should like to say a word about. You have listened so patiently, sir, to my lectures on the science of sciences that you will not refuse to hear the last. A good deal of importance has been attached to Mrs Drabdump's oversleeping herself by half an hour. It happens that this (like the innocent fog which has also been made responsible for much) is a purely accidental and irrelevant circumstance. In all works on inductive logic it is thoroughly recognized that only some of the circumstances of a phenomenon are of its essence and causally interconnected; there is always a certain proportion of heterogeneous accompaniments which have no intimate relation whatever with the phenomenon. Yet so crude is as yet the comprehension of the science of evidence, that every feature of the phenomenon under investigation is made equally important, and sought to be linked with the chain of evidence. To attempt to explain everything is always the mark of the tiro. The fog and Mrs Drabdump's oversleeping herself were mere accidents. There are always these irrelevant accompaniments, and the true scientist allows for this element of (so to speak) chemically unrelated detail. Even I never counted on the unfortunate series of accidental phenomena which have led to Mortlake's implication in a network of suspicion. On the other hand, the fact that my servant Jane, who usually goes about ten, left a few minutes earlier on the night of December 3rd, so that she didn't know of Constant's visit, was a relevant accident. In fact, just as the art of the artist or the editor consists largely in knowing what to leave out, so does the art of the scientific detector of crime consist in knowing what details to ignore. In short, to explain everything is to explain too much. And too much is worse than too little.

'To return to my experiment. My success exceeded my wildest dreams. None had an inkling of the truth. The insolubility of the Big Bow Mystery teased the acutest minds in Europe and the civilized world. That a man could have been murdered in a thoroughly inaccessible room savoured of the ages of magic. The redoubtable Wimp, who had been blazoned as my successor, fell back on the theory of suicide. The mystery would have slept till my death, but—I fear—for my own ingenuity. I tried to stand outside myself, and to look at the crime with the eyes of another, or of my old self. I found the work of art so perfect as to leave only one sublimely simple solution. The very terms of the problem were so inconceivable that, had I not been the murderer, I should have suspected myself, in conjunction of course with Mrs Drabdump. The first persons to enter the room would have seemed to me guilty. I wrote at once (in a disguised hand and over the signature of "One Who Looks Through His Own Spectacles") to the *Pell Mell Press* to suggest this. By associating myself thus with Mrs Drabdump I made it difficult for people to dissociate the two who entered the room together. To dash a half-truth in the world's eyes is the surest way of blinding it altogether. This pseudonymous letter of mine I contradicted in my own name the next day, and in the course of the long letter which I was tempted to write I adduced fresh evidence against the theory of suicide. I was disgusted with the open verdict, and wanted men to be up and doing and trying to find me out. I enjoyed the hunt more.

'Unfortunately, Wimp, set on the chase again by my own letter, by dint of persistent blundering, blundered into a track which—by a devilish tissue of coincidences I had neither fore-seen nor dreamt of—seemed to the world the true. Mortlake was arrested and condemned. Wimp had apparently crowned his reputation. This was too much. I had taken all this trouble merely to put a feather in Wimp's cap, whereas I had expected to shake his reputation by it. It was bad enough that an innocent man should suffer; but that Wimp should achieve a reputation he did not deserve, and overshadow all his predecessors by dint of a colossal mistake, this seemed to me intolerable. I have moved heaven and earth to get the verdict set aside and to save the prisoner; I have exposed the weakness of the evidence; I have had the world searched for the missing girl; I have petitioned and agitated. In vain. I have failed. Now I play my last card. As the overweening

Wimp could not be allowed to go down to posterity as the solver of this terrible mystery, I decided that the condemned man might just as well profit by his exposure. That is the reason I make the exposure tonight, before it is too late to save Mortlake.'

'So that is the reason?' said the Home Secretary with a suspicion of mockery in his tones.

'The sole reason.'

Even as he spoke a deeper roar than ever penetrated the study. 'A Reprieve! Hooray! Hooray!' The whole street seemed to rock with earthquake, and the names of Grodman and Mortlake to be thrown up in a fiery jet. 'A Reprieve! A Reprieve!' The very windows rattled. And even above the roar rose the shrill voices of the news-boys: 'Reprieve of Mortlake! Mortlake reprieved!'

Grodman looked wonderingly towards the street. 'How do they know?' he murmured.

'Those evening papers are amazing.' Said the minister dryly. 'But I suppose they had everything ready in type for the contingency.' He turned to his secretary. 'Templeton, have you got down every word of Mr Grodman's confession?'

'Every word, sir.'

'Then bring in the cable you received just as Mr Grodman entered the house.'

Templeton went back into the outer room and brought back the cablegram that had been lying on the Minister's writing-table when Grodman came in. The Home Secretary silently handed it to his visitor. It was from the Chief of Police of Melbourne, announcing that Jessie Dymond had just arrived in that city in a sailing vessel, ignorant of all that had occurred, and had been immediately despatched back to England, having made a statement entirely corroborating the theory of the defence.

'Pending further inquiries into this,' said the Home Secretary, not without appreciation of the grim humour of the situation as he glanced at Grodman's ashen cheeks, 'I had already re-prieved the prisoner. Mr Templeton went out to dispatch the messenger to the governor of Newgate as you entered this room. Mr Wimp's card-castle would have tumbled to pieces without your assistance. Your still undiscoverable crime would have shaken his reputation as you intended.'

A sudden explosion shook the room and blent with the cheers of the populace. Grodman had shot himself—very scientifically—in the heart. He fell at the Home Secretary's feet, stone dead.

Some of the working men who had been standing waiting by the shafts of the hansom helped to bear the stretcher.

THE END

THE MURDERS IN THE RUE MORGUE

BY

EDGAR ALLAN POE

INTRODUCTION

THE historical significance of 'The Murders in the Rue Morgue', first published in 1841, and its recognition as the first detective story, can be judged from the presence of so many elements that would come to define the genre of detective fiction. A mother and daughter are found brutally murdered in a room locked from the inside; and an arrest is made. But the reclusive Chevalier C. Auguste Dupin, accompanied by the unnamed narrator, identifies the completely unexpected perpetrator by a process of logical reasoning—called 'ratiocination' by Poe—based on the observation of significant, but seemingly irrelevant, facts. So, we find the brilliant detective, the less-than-brilliant narrator friend, the crime that baffles the police, the wrongly arrested suspect, the locked room, and the unexpected but logical solution, deduced from clues presented throughout the story. Writing in 1934, G. K. Chesterton, the creator of priest-detective Father Brown, was unequivocal in his estimation of the story's importance:

'I do not think that the standard set by a certain Mr Edgar A[llan] Poe in a story called "The Murders of [sic] the Rue Morgue", has ever been definitely and indisputably surpassed. The two essentials of such a story are that the logic should be clear and yet the climax should be unexpected.'

Dupin exemplifies many features that would come to distinguish the detective figure in the work of subsequent writers. He is observant, intelligent, arrogant and contemptuous of the police; during the course of this investigation he remarks: 'In fact, the facility with which I shall arrive, or have arrived, at the solution of this mystery, is in direct ratio of its apparent insolubility in the eyes of the police.' His motivation for investigating 'The Murders in the Rue Morgue' foreshadows that of many later amateur sleuths: he does it for amusement. Although there is little in the way of physical description or personal detail, we learn that he comes from an illustrious but impoverished family and lives in 'a time-eaten and grotesque mansion, long deserted through superstition', paid for by his nameless companion. Because they are both 'enamoured of the Night for her own sake', they close the 'massy shutters' as soon as dawn breaks and light 'a couple of tapers which . . . give out only the ghastliest and feeblest of rays' and they venture out only at night, 'amid the wild lights and shadows of the populous city'. This gothic atmosphere is further heightened by the description of the gruesome Rue Morgue murder scene.

Also destined to become a recurrent feature of much subsequent detective fiction, the detective's companion acts as a nameless narrator, but also fulfils an important practical function. As the detective explains his observations and deductions to him—and this figure is almost always male—so the writer explains to the reader. The most famous example of the companion/narrator is undoubtedly Dr Watson, the chronicler of the investigations of Sherlock Holmes. In fact, so inextricably linked with this literary device did Dr Watson become, that his name is accepted shorthand for this type of character: 'the Watson'.

The room in which the Rue Morgue victims are found is locked from the inside, thereby making the killer's escape seemingly impossible. Although an important consideration in the elucidation of the crime, the plot device here does not merit the prominence it was later to receive when it eventually produced an entire sub-section of the genre, in which the explanation of the sealed room was as central as, and frequently more baffling than, the identity of the killer.

Further, the presence of both a wrongly arrested suspect and an unexpected solution also became regular features in subsequent detective fiction, although neither is a prerequisite. The former adds urgency, and, frequently, an emotional dimension, while the latter confounds reader expectation, a ploy which, as the genre developed, became almost its *raison d'être*.

Dupin appeared in only two further investigations: a murder, based on a true story, in 'The Mystery of Marie Rogêt' (1842) and a burglary in the shortest of the three stories, 'The Purloined Letter' (1844).

J.C.

What song the Syrens sang, or what name Achilles assumed when he hid himself among women, although puzzling questions, are not beyond all conjecture.

—Sir Thomas Browne

THE mental features discoursed of as the analytical, are, in themselves, but little susceptible of analysis. We appreciate them only in their effects. We know of them, among other things, that they are always to their possessor, when inordinately possessed, a source of the liveliest enjoyment. As the strong man exults in his physical ability, delighting in such exercises as call his muscles into action, so glories the analyst in that moral activity which *disentangles*. He derives pleasure from even the most trivial occupations bringing his talent into play. He is fond of enigmas, of conundrums, of hieroglyphics; exhibiting in his solutions of each a degree of *acumen* which appears to the ordinary apprehension preternatural. His results, brought about by the very soul and essence of method, have, in truth, the whole air of intuition.

The faculty of re-solution is possibly much invigorated by mathematical study, and especially by that highest branch of it which, unjustly, and merely on account of its retrograde operations, has been called, as if *par excellence*, analysis. Yet to calculate is not in itself to analyse. A chess-player, for example, does the one without effort at the other. It follows that the game of chess, in its effects upon mental character, is greatly misunderstood. I am not now writing a treatise, but simply prefacing a somewhat peculiar narrative by observations very much at random; I will, therefore, take occasion to assert that the higher powers of the reflective intellect are more decidedly and more usefully tasked by the unostentatious game of draughts than by all the elaborate frivolity of chess. In this latter, where the pieces have different and *bizarre* motions, with various and variable values, what is only complex is mistaken (a not unusual error) for what is profound. The *attention* is here called powerfully into play. If it flag for an instant, an oversight is committed resulting in injury or defeat. The possible moves being not only manifold but involute, the chances of such oversights are multiplied; and in nine cases out of ten it is the more concentrative rather than the more acute player who conquers. In draughts, on the contrary, where the moves are *unique* and have but little variation, the probabilities of inadvertence are diminished, and the mere attention being left comparatively unemployed, what advantages are obtained by either party are obtained by superior *acumen*. To be less abstract—Let us suppose a game of draughts where the pieces are reduced to four kings, and where, of course, no oversight is to be expected. It is obvious that here the victory can be decided (the players being at all equal) only by some *recherché* movement, the result of some strong exertion of the intellect. Deprived of ordinary resources, the analyst throws himself into the spirit of his opponent, identifies himself therewith, and not unfrequently sees thus, at a glance, the sole methods (sometime indeed absurdly simple ones) by which he may seduce into error or hurry into miscalculation.

Whist has long been noted for its influence upon what is termed the calculating power; and men of the highest order of intellect have been known to take an apparently unaccountable delight in it, while eschewing chess as frivolous. Beyond doubt there is nothing of a similar nature so greatly tasking the faculty of analysis. The best chessplayer in Christendom *may* be little more than the best player of chess; but proficiency in whist implies capacity for success in all those more important undertakings where mind struggles with mind. When I say proficiency, I mean that perfection in the game which includes a comprehension of *all* the sources whence legitimate advantage may be derived. These are not only manifold but multiform, and lie frequently among recesses of thought altogether inaccessible to the ordinary understanding. To observe attentively is to remember distinctly; and, so far, the concentrative chess-player will do very well at whist; while the rules of Hoyle (themselves based upon the mere mechanism of the game) are sufficiently and generally comprehensible. Thus to have a retentive memory, and to proceed by 'the book', are points commonly regarded as the sum total of good playing. But it is in matters beyond the limits of mere rule that the skill of the analyst is evinced. He makes, in silence, a host of observations and inferences. So, perhaps, do his companions; and the difference in the extent of the information obtained lies not so much in the validity of the inference as in the quality of the observation. The necessary knowledge is that of *what* to observe. Our player confines himself not at all; nor, because the game is the object, does he reject deductions from things external to the game. He examines the countenance of his partner, comparing it carefully with that of each of his opponents. He considers the mode of assorting the cards in each hand; often counting trump by trump, and honour by honour, through the glances bestowed by their holders upon each. He notes every variation of face as the play progresses, gathering a fund of thought from the differences in the expression of certainty, of surprise, of triumph, or of chagrin. From the manner of gathering up a trick he judges whether the person taking it can make another in the suit. He recognises what is played through feint, by the air with which it is thrown upon the table. A casual or inadvertent word; the accidental dropping or turning of a card, with the accompanying anxiety or carelessness in regard to its concealment; the counting of the tricks, with the order of their arrangement; embarrassment, hesitation, eagerness or trepidation—all afford, to his apparently intuitive perception, indications of the true state of affairs. The first two or three rounds having been played, he is in full possession of the contents of each hand, and thenceforward puts down his cards with as absolute a precision of purpose as if the rest of the party had turned outward the faces of their own.

The analytical power should not be confounded with ample ingenuity; for while the analyst is necessarily ingenious, the ingenious man is often remarkably incapable of analysis. The constructive or combining power by which ingenuity is usually manifested, and to which the phrenologists (I believe erroneously) have assigned a separate organ, supposing it a primitive faculty, has been so frequently seen in those whose intellect bordered otherwise upon idiocy, as to have attracted general observation among writers on morals. Between ingenuity and the analytic ability there exists a difference far greater, indeed, than that between the fancy and the imagination, but of a character very strictly analogous. It will be found, in fact, that the ingenious are always fanciful, and the *truly* imaginative never otherwise than analytic.

The narrative which follows will appear to the reader somewhat in the light of a commentary upon the propositions just advanced.

Residing in Paris during the spring and part of the summer of 18—, I there became acquainted with a Monsieur C. Auguste Dupin. This young gentleman was of an excellent— indeed of an illustrious family, but, by a variety of untoward events, had been reduced to such poverty that the energy of his character succumbed beneath it, and he ceased to bestir himself in the world, or to care for the retrieval of his fortunes. By courtesy of his creditors, there still remained in his possession a small remnant of his patrimony; and, upon the income arising from this, he managed, by means of a rigorous economy, to procure the necessaries of life, without troubling himself about its superfluities. Books, indeed, were his sole luxuries, and in Paris these are easily obtained.

Our first meeting was at an obscure library in the Rue Montmartre, where the accident of our both being in search of the same very rare and very remarkable volume brought us into closer communion. We saw each other again and again. I was deeply interested in the little family history which he detailed to me with all that candour which a Frenchman indulges whenever mere self is his theme. I was astonished, too, at the vast extent of his reading; and, above all, I felt my soul enkindled within me by the wild fervour and the vivid freshness of his imagination. Seeking in Paris the objects I then sought, I felt that the society of such a man would be to me a treasure beyond price; and this feeling I frankly confided to him. It was at length arranged that we should live together during my stay in the city; and as my worldly circumstances were somewhat less embarrassed than his own, I was permitted to be at the expense of renting, and furnishing in a style which suited the rather fantastic gloom of our common temper, a time-eaten and grotesque mansion, long deserted through superstitions into which we did not inquire, and tottering to its fall in a retired and desolate portion of the Faubourg St Germain.

Had the routine of our life at this place been known to the world, we should have been regarded as madmen—although, perhaps, as madmen of a harmless nature. Our seclusion was perfect. We admitted no visitors. Indeed the locality of our retirement had been carefully kept a secret from my own former associates; and it had been many years since Dupin had ceased to know or be known in Paris. We existed within ourselves alone.

It was a freak of fancy in my friend (for what else shall I call it?) to be enamoured of the Night for her own sake; and into this *bizarrerie*, as into all his others, I quietly fell; giving myself up to his wild whims with a perfect *abandon*. The sable divinity would not herself dwell with us always; but we could counterfeit her presence. At the first dawn of the morning we closed all the messy shutters of our old building; lighting a couple of tapers which, strongly perfumed, threw out only the ghastliest and feeblest of rays. By the aid of these we then busied our souls in dreams—reading, writing, or conversing, until warned by the clock of the advent of the true Darkness. Then we sallied forth into the streets arm in arm, continuing the topics of the day, or roaming far and wide until a late hour, seeking, amid the wild lights and shadows of the populous city, that infinity of mental excitement which quiet observation can afford.

At such times I could not help remarking and admiring (although from his rich ideality I had been prepared to expect it) a peculiar analytic ability in Dupin. He seemed, too, to take an eager delight in its exercise—if not exactly in its display— and did not hesitate to confess the pleasure thus derived. He boasted to me, with a low chuckling laugh, that most men, in respect to himself, wore windows in their bosoms, and was wont to follow up such assertions by direct and very startling proofs of his intimate knowledge of my own. His manner at these moments was frigid and abstract; his eyes were vacant in expression; while his voice, usually a rich tenor, rose into a treble which would have sounded petulantly but for the deliberateness and entire distinctness of the enunciation. Observing him in these moods, I often dwelt meditatively upon the old philosophy of the Bi-Part Soul, and amused myself with the fancy of a double Dupin—the creative and the resolvent.

Let it not be supposed, from what I have just said, that I am detailing any mystery, or penning any romance. What I have described in the Frenchman was merely the result of an excited or perhaps of a diseased intelligence. But of the character of his remarks at the periods in question an example will best convey the idea.

We were strolling one night down a long dirty street in the vicinity of the Palais Royal. Being both, apparently, occupied with thought, neither of us had spoken a syllable for fifteen minutes at least. All at once Dupin broke forth with these words:

'He is a very little fellow, that's true, and would do better for the *Théâtre des Variétés*.'

'There can be no doubt of that,' I replied unwittingly, and not at first observing (so much had I been absorbed in reflection) the extraordinary manner in which the speaker had chimed in with my meditations. In an instant afterward I recollected myself, and my astonishment was profound.

'Dupin,' said I, gravely, 'this is beyond my comprehension. I do not hesitate to say that I am amazed, and can scarcely credit my senses. How was it possible you should know I was thinking of—?' Here I paused, to ascertain beyond a doubt whether he really knew of whom I thought.

'—of Chantilly,' said he, 'why do you pause? You were remarking to yourself that his diminutive figure unfitted him for tragedy.'

This was precisely what had formed the subject of my reflections. Chantilly was a *quondam* cobbler of the Rue St Denis, who, becoming stage-mad, had attempted the *rôle* of Xerxes, in Crébillon's tragedy so called, and been notoriously Pasquinaded for his pains.

'Tell me, for Heaven's sake,' I exclaimed, 'the method—if method there is—by which you have been enabled to fathom my soul in this matter.' In fact I was even more startled than I would have been willing to express.

'It was the fruiterer,' replied my friend, 'who brought you to the conclusion that the mender of soles was not of sufficient height for Xerxes *et id genus omne*.'

'The fruiterer!—you astonish me—I know no fruiterer whomsoever.'

'The man who ran up against you as we entered the street— it may have been fifteen minutes ago.'

I now remembered that, in fact, a fruiterer, carrying upon his head a large basket of apples, had nearly thrown me down, by accident, as we passed from the Rue C— into the thoroughfare where we stood; but what this had to do with Chantilly I could not possibly understand.

There was not a particle of *charlatanerie* about Dupin. 'I will explain,' he said, 'and that you may comprehend all clearly, we will first retrace the course of your meditations, from the moment in which I spoke to you until that of the *rencontre* with the fruiterer in question. The larger links of the chain run thus—Chantilly, Orion, Dr Nichols, Epicurus, Stereotomy, the street stones, the fruiterer.'

There are few persons who have not, at some period of their lives, amused themselves in retracing the steps by which particular conclusions of their own minds have been attained. The occupation is often full of interest and he who attempts it for the first time is astonished by the apparently illimitable distance and incoherence between the starting-point and the goal. What, then, must have been my amazement when I heard the Frenchman speak what he had just spoken, and when I could not help acknowledging that he had spoken the truth. He continued:

'We had been talking of horses, if I remember aright, just before leaving the Rue C—. This was the last subject we discussed. As we crossed into this street, a fruiterer, with a large basket upon his head, brushing quickly past us, thrust you upon a pile of paving stones collected at a spot where the causeway is undergoing repair. You stepped upon one of the loose fragments, slipped, slightly strained your ankle, appeared vexed or sulky, muttered a few words, turned to look at the pile, and then proceeded in silence. I was not particularly attentive to what you did; but observation has become with me, of late, a species of necessity.

'You kept your eyes upon the ground—glancing, with a petulant expression, at the holes and ruts in the pavement (so that I saw you were still thinking of the stones), until we reached the little alley called Lamartine, which has been paved, by way of experiment, with the overlapping and riveted blocks. Here your countenance brightened up, and, perceiving your lips move, I could not doubt that you murmured the word "stereotomy", a term very affectedly applied to this species of pavement. I knew that you could not say to yourself "stereotomy" without being brought to think of atomies, and thus of the theories of Epicurus; and since, when we discussed this subject not very long ago, I mentioned to you how singularly, yet with how little notice, the vague guesses of that noble Greek had met with confirmation in the late nebular cosmogony, I felt that you could not avoid casting your eyes upward to the great *nebula* in Orion, and I certainly expected that you would do so. You did look up; and I was now assured that I had correctly followed your steps. But in that bitter *tirade* upon Chantilly, which appeared in yesterday's *Musée*, the satirist, making some disgraceful allusions to the cobbler's change of name upon assuming the buskin, quoted a Latin line about which we have often conversed. I mean the line: *Perdidit antiquum litera sonum.*

'I had told you that this was in reference to Orion, formerly written Urion; and, from certain pungencies connected with this explanation, I was aware that you could not have forgotten it. It was clear, therefore, that you would not fail to combine the two ideas of Orion and Chantilly. That you did combine them I saw by the character of the smile which passed over your lips. You thought of the poor cobbler's immolation. So far, you had been stooping in your gait; but now I saw you draw yourself up to your full height. I was then sure that you reflected upon the diminutive figure of Chantilly. At this point I interrupted your meditations to remark that as, in fact, he was a very little fellow—that Chantilly—he would do better at the *Théâtre des Variétés*.'

Not long after this, we were looking over an evening edition of the *Gazette des Tribunaux*, when the following paragraphs arrested our attention:

EXTRAORDINARY MURDERS

This morning, about three o'clock, the inhabitants of the Quartier St Roch were aroused from sleep by a succession of terrific shrieks, issuing, apparently, from the fourth storey of a house in the Rue Morgue, known to be in the sole occupancy of one Madame L'Espanaye, and her daughter Mademoiselle Camille L'Espanaye. After some delay, occasioned by a fruitless attempt to procure admission in the usual manner, the gateway was broken in with a crowbar, and eight or ten of the neighbours entered accompanied by two *gendarmes*. By this time the cries had ceased; but, as the party rushed up the first flight of stairs, two or more rough voices in angry contention were distinguished and seemed to proceed from the upper part of the house. As the second landing was reached, these sounds, also, had ceased and everything remained perfectly quiet. The party spread themselves and hurried from room to room. Upon arriving at a large back chamber in the fourth story (the door of which, being found locked, with the key inside, was forced open), a spectacle presented itself which struck every one present not less with horror than with astonishment.

The apartment was in the wildest disorder—the furniture broken and thrown about in all directions. There was only one bedstead; and from this the bed had been removed, and thrown into the middle of the floor. On a chair lay a razor, besmeared with blood. On the hearth were two or three long and thick tresses of grey human hair, also dabbled in blood, and seeming to have been pulled out by the roots. Upon the floor were found four Napoleons, an earring of topaz, three large silver spoons, three smaller of *métal d'Alger*, and two bags, containing nearly four thousand francs in gold. The drawers of a *bureau*, which stood in one corner, were open, and had been, apparently, rifled, although many articles still remained in them. A small iron safe was discovered under the *bed* (not under the bedstead). It was open, with the key still in the door. It had no contents beyond a few old letters, and other papers of little consequence.

Of Madame L'Espanaye no traces were here seen; but an unusual quantity of soot being observed in the fireplace, a search was made in the chimney, and (horrible to relate!) the corpse of the daughter, head downward, was dragged therefrom; it having been thus forced up the narrow aperture for a considerable distance. The body was quite warm. Upon examining it, many excoriations were perceived, no doubt occasioned by the violence with which it had been thrust up and disengaged. Upon the face were many severe scratches, and, upon the throat, dark bruises and deep indentations of fingernails, as if the deceased had been throttled to death.

After a thorough investigation of every portion of the house, without farther discovery, the party made its way into a small paved yard in the rear of the building, where lay the corpse of the old lady, with her throat so entirely cut that, upon an attempt to raise her, the head fell off. The body, as well as the head, was fearfully mutilated—the former so much so as scarcely to retain any semblance of humanity.

To this horrible mystery there is not as yet, we believe, the slightest clew.

The next day's paper had these additional particulars:

THE TRAGEDY IN THE RUE MORGUE

Many individuals have been examined in relation to this most extraordinary and frightful affair [the word 'affaire' has not yet, in France, that levity of import which it conveys with us], but nothing whatever has transpired to throw light upon it. We give below all the material testimony elicited.

Pauline Dubourg, laundress, deposes that she has known both the deceased for three years, having washed for them during that period. The old lady and her daughter seemed on good terms—very affectionate towards each other. They were excellent pay. Could not speak in regard to their mode or means of living. Believed that Madame L. told fortunes for a living. Was reputed to have money put by. Never met any persons in the house when she called for the clothes or took them home. Was sure that they had no servant in employ. There appeared to be no furniture in any part of the building except in the fourth storey.

Pierre Moreau, tobacconist, deposes that he has been in the habit of selling small quantities of tobacco and snuff to Madame L'Espanaye for nearly four years. Was born in the neighbourhood, and has always resided there. The deceased and her daughter had occupied the house in which the corpses were found for more than six years. It was formerly occupied by a jeweller, who under-let the upper rooms to various persons. The house was the property of Madame L. She became dissatisfied with the abuse of the premises by her tenant, and moved into them herself, refusing to let any portion. The old lady was childish. Witness had seen the daughter some five or six times during the six years. The two lived an exceedingly retired life—were reputed to have money. Had heard it said among the neighbours that Madame L. told fortunes—did not believe it. Had never seen any person enter the door except the old lady and her daughter, a porter once or twice, and a physician some eight or ten times.

Many other persons, neighbours, gave evidence to the same effect. No one was spoken of as frequenting the house. It was not known whether there were any living connexions of Madame L. and her daughter. The shutters of the front windows were seldom opened. Those in the rear were always closed, with the exception of the large back room, fourth storey. The house was a good house—not very old.

Isidore Muset, *gendarme*, deposes that he was called to the house about three o'clock in the morning, and found some twenty or thirty persons at the gateway, endeavouring to gain admittance. Forced it open, at length, with a bayonet—not with a crowbar. Had but little difficulty in getting it open, on account of its being a double or folding gate, and bolted neither at bottom nor top. The shrieks were continued until the gate was forced—and then suddenly ceased. They seemed to be screams of some person (or persons) in great agony—were loud and drawn out, not short and quick. Witness led the way up stairs. Upon reaching the first landing, heard two voices in loud and angry contention—the one a gruff voice, the other much shriller—a very strange voice. Could distinguish some words of the former, which was that of a Frenchman. Was positive that it was not a woman's voice. Could distinguish the words '*sacré*' and '*diable*'. The shrill voice was that of a foreigner. Could not be sure whether it was the voice of a man or of a woman. Could not make out what was said, but believed the language to be Spanish. The state of the room and of the bodies was described by this witness as we described them yesterday.

Henri Duval, a neighbour, and by trade a silversmith, deposes that he was one of the party who first entered the house. Corroborates the testimony of Muset in general. As soon as they forced an entrance, they reclosed the door, to keep out the crowd, which collected very fast, notwithstanding the lateness of the hour. The shrill voice, this witness thinks, was that of an Italian. Was certain it was not French. Could not be sure that it was a man's voice. It might have been a woman's. Was not acquainted with the Italian language. Could not distinguish the words, but was convinced by the intonation that the speaker was an Italian. Knew Madame L. and her daughter. Had conversed with both frequently. Was sure that the shrill voice was not that of either of the deceased.

— *Odenheimer, restaurateur*. This witness volunteered his testimony. Not speaking French, was examined through an interpreter. Is a native of Amsterdam. Was passing the house at the time of the shrieks. They lasted for several minutes—probably ten. They were long and loud—very awful and distressing. Was one of those who entered the building. Corroborated the previous evidence in every respect but one.

Was sure that the shrill voice was that of a man—of a Frenchman. Could not distinguish the words uttered. They were loud and quick—unequal—spoken apparently in fear as well as in anger. The voice was harsh—not so much shrill as harsh. Could not call it a shrill voice. The gruff voice said repeatedly '*sacré*', '*diable*', and once '*mon Dieu*'.

Jules Mignaud, banker, of the firm of Mignaud et Fils, Rue Deloraine. Is the elder Mignaud. Madame L'Espanaye had some property. Had opened an account with his banking house in the spring of the year — (eight years previously). Made frequent deposits in small sums. Had checked for nothing until the third day before her death, when she took out in person the sum of 4000 francs. This sum was paid in gold, and a clerk went home with the money.

Adolphe Le Bon, clerk to Mignaud et Fils, deposes that on the day in question, about noon, he accompanied Madame L'Espanaye to her residence with the 4000 francs, put up in two bags. Upon the door being opened, Mademoiselle L. appeared and took from his hands one of the bags, while the old lady relieved him of the other. He then bowed and departed. Did not see any person in the street at the time. It is a bye-street—very lonely.

William Bird, tailor deposes that he was one of the party who entered the house. Is an Englishman. Has lived in Paris two years. Was one of the first to ascend the stairs. Heard the voices in contention. The gruff voice was that of a Frenchman. Could make out several words, but cannot now remember all. Heard distinctly '*sacré*' and '*mon Dieu*'. There was a sound at the moment as if of several persons struggling—a scraping and scuffling sound. The shrill voice was very loud—louder than the gruff one. Is sure that it was not the voice of an Englishman. Appeared to be that of a German. Might have been a woman's voice. Does not understand German.

Four of the above-named witnesses, being recalled, deposed that the door of the chamber in which was found the body of Mademoiselle L. was locked on the inside when the party reached it. Everything was perfectly silent—no groans or noises of any kind. Upon forcing the door no person was seen. The windows, both of the back and front room, were down and firmly fastened from within. A door between the two rooms was closed, but not locked. The door leading from the front room into the passage was locked, with the key on the inside. A small room in the front of the house, on the fourth storey, at the head of the passage was open, the door being ajar. This room was crowded with old beds, boxes, and so forth. These were carefully removed and searched. There was not an inch of any portion of the house which was not carefully searched. Sweeps were sent up and down the chimneys. The house was a four storey one, with garrets (*mansardes*). A trap-door on the roof was nailed down very securely—did not appear to have been opened for years. The time elapsing between the hearing of the voices in contention and the breaking open of the room door was variously stated by the witnesses. Some made it as short as three minutes—some as long as five. The door was opened with difficulty.

Alfonzo Garcio, undertaker, deposes that he resides in the Rue Morgue. Is a native of Spain. Was one of the party who entered the house. Did not proceed up stairs. Is nervous, and was apprehensive of the consequences of agitation. Heard the voices in contention. The gruff voice was that of a Frenchman. Could not distinguish what was said. The shrill voice was that of an Englishman—is sure of this. Does not understand the English language, but judges by the intonation.

Alberto Montani, confectioner, deposes that he was among the first to ascend the stairs. Heard the voices in question. The gruff voice was that of a Frenchman. Distinguished several words. The speaker appeared to be expostulating. Could not make out the words of the shrill voice. Spoke quick and unevenly. Thinks it the voice of a Russian. Corroborates the general testimony. Is an Italian. Never conversed with a native of Russia.

Several witnesses, recalled, here testified that the chimneys of all the rooms on the fourth storey were too narrow to admit the passage of a human being. By 'sweeps' were meant cylindrical sweeping brushes, such as are employed by those who clean chimneys. These brushes were passed up and down every flue in the house. There is no back passage by which anyone could have descended while the party proceeded up stairs. The body of Mademoiselle L'Espanaye was so firmly wedged in the chimney that it could not be got down until four or five of the party united their strength.

Paul Dumas, physician, deposes that he was called to view the bodies about day-break. They were both then lying on the sacking of the bedstead in the chamber where Mademoiselle L. was found. The corpse of the young lady was much bruised and excoriated. The fact that it had been thrust up the chimney would sufficiently account for these appearances. The throat was greatly chafed. There were several deep scratches just below the chin, together with a series of livid spots which were evidently the impression of fingers. The face was fearfully discoloured, and the eye-balls protruded. The tongue had been partially bitten through. A large bruise was discovered upon the pit of the stomach, produced, apparently, by the pressure of a knee. In the opinion of M. Dumas, Mademoiselle L'Espanaye had been throttled to death by some person or persons unknown. The corpse of the mother was horribly mutilated. All the bones of the right leg and arm were more or less shattered. The left *tibia* much splintered, as well as all the ribs of the left side. Whole body dreadfully bruised and discoloured. It was not possible to say how the injuries had been inflicted. A heavy club of wood, or a broad bar of iron—a chair—any large, heavy, and obtuse weapon would have produced such results, if wielded by the hands of a very powerful man. No woman could have inflicted the blows with any weapon. The head of the deceased, when seen by witness, was entirely separated from the body, and was also greatly shattered. The throat had evidently been cut with some very sharp instrument—probably with a razor.

Alexandre Etienne, surgeon, was called with M. Dumas to view the bodies. Corroborated the testimony, and the opinions of M. Dumas.

Nothing farther of importance was elicited, although several other persons were examined. A murder so mysterious, and so perplexing in all its particulars, was never before committed in Paris—if indeed a murder has been committed at all. The police are entirely at fault—an unusual occurrence in affairs of this nature. There is not, however, the shadow of a clew apparent.

The evening edition of the paper stated that the greatest excitement still continued in the Quartier St Roch—that the premises in question had been carefully re-searched, and fresh examinations of witnesses instituted, but all to no purpose. A postscript, however, mentioned that Adolphe Le Bon had been arrested and imprisoned—although nothing appeared to criminate him, beyond the facts already detailed.

Dupin seemed singularly interested in the progress of this affair—at least so I judged from his manner, for he made no comments. It was only after the announcement that Le Bon had been imprisoned that he asked me my opinion respecting the murders.

I could merely agree with all Paris in considering them an insoluble mystery. I saw no means by which it would be possible to trace the murderer.

'We must not judge of the means,' said Dupin, 'by this shell of an examination. The Parisian police, so much extolled for *acumen*, are cunning, but no more. There is no method in their proceedings beyond the method of the moment. They make a vast parade of measures; but, not unfrequently, these are so ill adapted to the objects proposed, as to put us in mind of Monsieur Jourdain's calling for his *robe-de-chambre—pour mieux entendre la musique.* The results attained by them are not unfrequently surprising, but, for the most part, are brought about by simple diligence and activity. When these qualities are unavailing, their schemes fail. Vidocq, for example, was a good guesser and a persevering man. But, without educated thought, he erred continually by the very intensity of his investigations. He impaired his vision by holding the object too close. He might see, perhaps, one or two points with unusual clearness, but in so doing he, necessarily, lost sight of the matter as a whole. Thus there is such a thing as being too profound. Truth is not always in a well. In fact, as regards the more important knowledge, I do believe that she is invariably superficial. The depth lies in the valleys where we seek her, and not upon the mountain-tops where she is found. The modes and sources of this kind of error are well typified in the contemplation of the heavenly bodies. To look at a star by glances—to view it in a side-long way, by turning toward it the exterior portions of the *retina* (more susceptible of feeble impressions of light than the interior), is to behold the star distinctly—is to have the best appreciation of its lustre— a lustre which grows dim just in proportion as we turn our vision *fully* upon it. A greater number of rays actually fall upon the eye in the latter case, but, in the former, there is the more refined capacity for comprehension. By undue profundity we perplex and enfeeble thought; and it is possible to make even Venus herself vanish from the firmament by a scrutiny too sustained, too concentrated, or too direct.

'As for these murders, let us enter into some examinations for ourselves, before we make up an opinion respecting them. An inquiry will afford us amusement' [I thought this an odd term, so applied, but said nothing] 'and, besides, Le Bon once rendered me a service for which I am not ungrateful. We will go and see the premises with our own eyes. I know G—, the Prefect of Police, and shall have no difficulty in obtaining the necessary permission.'

The permission was obtained, and we proceeded at once to the Rue Morgue. This is one of those miserable thoroughfares which intervene between the Rue Richelieu and the Rue St Roch. It was late in the afternoon when we reached it; as this quarter is at a great distance from that in which we resided. The house was readily found; for there were still many persons gazing up at the closed shutters, with an objectless curiosity, from the opposite side of the way. It was an ordinary Parisian house, with a gateway, on one side of which was a glazed watch-box, with a sliding panel in the window, indicating a *loge de concierge*. Before going in we walked up the street, turned down an alley, and then, again turning, passed in the rear of the building—Dupin, meanwhile examining the whole neighbourhood, as well as the house, with a minuteness of attention for which I could see no possible object.

Retracing our steps, we came again to the front of the dwelling, rang, and, having shown our credentials, were admitted by the agents in charge. We went upstairs—into the chamber where the body of Mademoiselle L'Espanaye had been found, and where both the deceased still lay. The disorders of the room had, as usual, been suffered to exist. I saw nothing beyond what had been stated in the *Gazette des Tribunaux*. Dupin scrutinized everything—not excepting the bodies of the victims. We then went into the other rooms, and into the yard; a *gendarme* accompanying us throughout. The examination occupied us until dark, when we took our departure. On our way home my companion stepped in for a moment at the office of one of the daily papers.

I have said that the whims of my friend were manifold, and that *Je les ménageais*: for this phrase there is no English equivalent. It was his humour, now, to decline all conversation on the subject of the murder, until about noon the next day. He then asked me, suddenly, if I had observed anything *peculiar* at the scene of the atrocity.

There was something in his manner of emphasizing the word 'peculiar' which caused me to shudder, without knowing why.

'No, nothing *peculiar*,' I said; 'nothing more, at least, than we both saw stated in the paper.'

'The *Gazette*,' he replied, 'has not entered, I fear, into the unusual horror of the thing. But dismiss the idle opinions of this print. It appears to me that this mystery is considered insoluble, for the very reason which should cause it to be regarded as easy of solution—I mean for the *outré* character of its features. The police are confounded by the seeming absence of motive—not for the murder itself—but for the atrocity of the murder. They are puzzled, too, by the seeming impossibility of reconciling the voices heard in contention, with the facts that no one was discovered upstairs but the assassinated Mademoiselle L'Espanaye, and that there were no means of egress without the notice of the party ascending. The wild disorder of the room; the corpse thrust, with the head downwards, up the chimney; the frightful mutilation of the body of the old lady; these considerations, with those just mentioned, and others which I need not mention, have sufficed to paralyse the powers by putting completely at fault the boasted *acumen* of the government agents. They have fallen into the gross but common error of confounding the unusual with the abstruse. But it is by these deviations from the plane of the ordinary that reason feels its way, if at all, in its search for the true. In investigations such as we are now pursuing, it should not be so much asked 'what has occurred?' as 'what has occurred that has never occurred before?' In fact, the facility with which I shall arrive, or have arrived, at the solution of this mystery, is in the direct ratio of its apparent insolubility in the eyes of the police.'

I stared at the speaker in mute astonishment.

'I am now awaiting,' continued he, looking toward the door of our apartment—'I am now awaiting a person who, although perhaps not the perpetrator of these butcheries, must have been in some measure implicated in their perpetration. Of the worst portion of the crimes committed, it is probable that he is innocent. I hope that I am right in this supposition; for upon it I build my expectation of reading the entire riddle. I look for the man here—in this room—every moment. It is true that he may not arrive; but the probability is that he will. Should he come, it will be necessary to detain him. Here are pistols; and we both know how to use them when occasion demands their use.'

I took the pistols, scarcely knowing what I did, or believing what I heard, while Dupin went on, very much as if in a soliloquy. I have already spoken of his abstract manner at such times. His discourse was addressed to myself; but his voice, although by no means loud, had that intonation which is commonly employed in speaking to someone at a great distance. His eyes, vacant in expression, regarded only the wall.

'That the voices heard in contention,' he said, 'by the party upon the stairs, were not the voices of the women themselves, was fully proved by the evidence. This relieves us of all doubt upon the question whether the old lady could have first destroyed the daughter and afterwards have committed suicide. I speak of this point chiefly for the sake of method; for the strength of Madame L'Espanaye would have been utterly unequal to the task of thrusting her daughter's corpse up the chimney as it was found; and the nature of the wounds upon her own person entirely preclude the idea of self-destruction. Murder, then, has been committed by some third party; and the voices of this third party were those heard in contention. Let me now advert—not to the whole testimony respecting these voices—but to what was *peculiar* in that testimony. Did you observe anything peculiar about it?'

I remarked that, while all the witnesses agreed in supposing the gruff voice to be that of a Frenchman, there was much disagreement in regard to the shrill, or, as one individual termed it, the harsh voice.

'That was the evidence itself,' said Dupin, 'but it was not the peculiarity of the evidence. You have observed nothing distinctive. Yet there *was* something to be observed. The witnesses, as you remark, agreed about the gruff voice; they were here unanimous. But in regard to the shrill voice, the peculiarity is—not that they disagreed—but that, while an Italian, an Englishman, a Spaniard, a Hollander and a Frenchman attempted to describe it, each one spoke of it as that *of a foreigner*. Each is sure that it was not the voice of one of his own countrymen. Each likens it—not to the voice of an individual of any nation with whose language he is conversant—but the converse. The Frenchman supposes it the voice of a Spaniard, and "might have distinguished some words *had he been acquainted with the Spanish*". The Dutchman maintains it to have been that of a Frenchman; but we find it stated that "*not understanding French this witness was examined through an interpreter*". The Englishman thinks it the voice of a German, and "*does not understand German*". The Spaniard "is sure" that it was that of an Englishman, but "judges by the intonation" altogether, "*as he has no knowledge of the English*". The Italian believes it the voice of a Russian, but "*has never conversed with a native of Russia*". A second Frenchman differs, moreover, with the first, and is positive that the voice was that of an Italian; but, *not being cognizant of that tongue*, is, like the Spaniard, "convinced by the intonation". Now, how strangely unusual must that voice have really been, about which such testimony as this *could* have been elicited!—in whose *tones*, even, denizens of the five great divisions of Europe could recognise nothing familiar! You will say that it might have been the voice of an Asiatic—of an African. Neither Asiatics nor Africans abound in Paris; but, without denying the inference, I will now merely call your attention to three points. The voice is termed by one witness "harsh rather than shrill". It is represented by two others to have been "quick and *unequal*". No words—no sounds resembling words—were by any witness mentioned as distinguishable.

'I know not,' continued Dupin, 'what impression I may have made, so far, upon your own understanding; but I do not hesitate to say that legitimate deductions even from this portion of the testimony—the portion respecting the gruff and shrill voices—are in themselves sufficient to engender a suspicion which should give direction to all farther progress in the investigation of the mystery. I said "legitimate deductions"; but my meaning is not thus fully expressed. I designed to imply that the deductions are the *sole* proper ones, and that the suspicion arises *inevitably* from them as the single result. What the suspicion is, however, I will not say just yet. I merely wish you to bear in mind that, with myself, it was sufficiently forcible to give a definite form—a certain tendency—to my inquiries in the chamber.

'Let us now transport ourselves, in fancy, to this chamber. What shall we first seek here? The means of egress employed by the murderers. It is not too much to say that neither of us believe in preternatural events. Madame and Mademoiselle L'Espanaye were not destroyed by spirits. The doers of the deed were material, and escaped materially. Then how? Fortunately, there is but one mode of reasoning upon the point, and that mode *must* lead us to a definite decision. Let us examine, each by each, the possible means of egress. It is clear that the assassins were in the room where Mademoiselle L'Espanaye was found, or at least in the room adjoining, when the party ascended the stairs. It is then only from these two apartments that we have to seek issues. The police have laid bare the floors, the ceilings, and the masonry of the walls, in every direction. No *secret* issues could have escaped their vigilance. But, not trusting to *their* eyes, I examined with my own. There were, then, no secret issues. Both doors leading from the rooms into the passage were securely locked, with the keys inside. Let us turn to the chimneys. These, although of ordinary width for some eight or ten feet above the hearths, will not admit, throughout their extent, the body of a large cat. The impossibility of egress, by means already stated, being thus absolute, we are reduced to the windows. Through those of the front room no one could have escaped without notice from the crowd in the street. The murderers *must* have passed, then, through those of the back room. Now, brought to this conclusion in so unequivocal a manner as we are, it is not our part, as reasoners, to reject it on account of apparent impossibilities. It is only left for us to prove that these apparent "impossibilities" are, in reality, not such.

'There are two windows in the chamber. One of them is unobstructed by furniture, and is wholly visible. The lower portion of the other is hidden from view by the head of the unwieldy bedstead which is thrust close up against it. The former was found securely fastened from within. It resisted the utmost force of those who endeavoured to raise it. A large gimlet-hole had been pierced in its frame to the left, and a very stout nail was found fitted therein, nearly to the head. Upon examining the other window, a similar nail was seen similarly fitted in it; and a vigorous attempt to raise this sash failed also. The police were now entirely satisfied that egress had not been in these directions. And, *therefore*, it was thought a matter of supererogation to withdraw the nails and open the windows.

'My own examination was somewhat more particular, and was so for the reason I have just given—because here it was, I knew, that all apparent impossibilities *must* be proved to be not such in reality.

'I proceeded to think thus—*a posteriori*. The murderers did escape from one of these windows. This being so, they could not have refastened the sashes from the inside, as they were found fastened—the consideration which put a stop, through its obviousness, to the scrutiny of the police in this quarter. Yet the sashes *were* fastened. They *must*, then, have the power of fastening themselves. There was no escape from this conclusion. I stepped to the unobstructed casement, withdrew the nail with some difficulty and attempted to raise the sash. It resisted all my efforts, as I had anticipated. A concealed spring must, I now know, exist; and this corroboration of my idea convinced me that my premises at least were correct, however mysterious still appeared the circumstances attending the nails. A careful search soon brought to light the hidden spring. I pressed it, and, satisfied with the discovery, forbore to upraise the sash.

'I now replaced the nail and regarded it attentively. A person passing out through this window might have reclosed it, and the spring would have caught—but the nail could not have been replaced. The conclusion was plain, and again narrowed in the field of my investigations. The assassins *must* have escaped through the other window. Supposing, then, the springs upon each sash to be the same, as was probable, there *must* be found a difference between the nails, or at least between the modes of their fixture. Getting upon the sacking of the bedstead, I looked over the head-board minutely at the second casement. Passing my hand down behind the board, I readily discovered and pressed the spring, which was, as I had supposed, identical in character with its neighbour. I now looked at the nail. It was as stout as the other, and apparently fitted in the same manner—driven in nearly up to the head.

'You will say that I was puzzled; but, if you think so, you must have misunderstood the nature of the inductions. To use a sporting phrase, I had not been once "at fault". The scent had never for an instant been lost. There was no flaw in any link of the chain. I had traced the secret to its ultimate result—and that result was *the nail.* It had, I say, in every respect, the appearance of its fellow in the other window; but this fact was an absolute nullity (conclusive us it might seem to be) when compared with the consideration that here, at this point, terminated the clew. "There *must* be something wrong," I said, "about the nail." I touched it; and the head, with about a quarter of an inch of the shank, came off in my fingers. The rest of the shank was in the gimlet-hole where it had been broken off. The fracture was an old one (for its edges were encrusted with rust), and had apparently been accomplished by the blow of a hammer, which had partially embedded, in the top of the bottom sash, the head portion of the nail. I now carefully replaced this head portion in the indentation whence I had taken it, and the resemblance to a perfect nail was complete—the fissure was invisible. Pressing the spring, I gently raised the sash for a few inches; the head went up with it, remaining firm in its bed. I closed the window, and the semblance of the whole nail was again perfect.

'The riddle, so far, was now unriddled. The assassin had escaped through the window which looked upon the bed. Dropping of its own accord upon his exit (or perhaps purposely closed), it had become fastened by the spring; and it was the retention of this spring which had been mistaken by the police for that of the nail—farther inquiry being thus considered unnecessary.

'The next question is that of the mode of descent. Upon this point I had been satisfied in my walk with you around the building. About five feet and a half from the casement in question there runs a lightning-rod. From this rod it would have been impossible for anyone to reach the window itself, to say nothing of entering it. I observed, however, that the shutters of the fourth story were of the peculiar kind called by Parisian carpenters *ferrades*—a kind rarely employed at the present day, but frequently seen upon very old mansions at Lyons and Bordeaux. They are in the form of an ordinary door (a single, not a folding door), except that the lower half is latticed or worked in open trellis—thus affording an excellent hold for the hands. In the present instance these shutters are fully three feet and a half broad. When we saw them from the rear of the house, they were both about half open—that is to say, they stood off at right angles from the wall. It is probable that the police, as well as myself, examined the back of the tenement; but, if so, in looking at these *ferrades* in the line of their breadth (as they must have done), they did not perceive this great breadth itself, or, at all events, failed to take it into due consideration. In fact, having once satisfied themselves that no egress could have been made in this quarter, they would naturally bestow here a very cursory examination. It was clear to me, however, that the shutter belonging to the window at the head of the bed would, if swung fully back to the wall, reach to within two feet of the lightning-rod. It was also evident that, by exertion of a very unusual degree of activity and courage, an entrance into the window, from the rod, might have been thus effected. By reaching to the distance of two feet and a half (we now suppose the shutter open to its whole extent) a robber might have taken a firm grasp upon the trellis-work. Letting go, then, his hold upon the rod, placing his feet securely against the wall and springing boldly from it, he might have swung the shutter so as to close it and, if we imagine the window open at the time, might even have swung himself into the room.

'I wish you to bear especially in mind that I have spoken of a *very* unusual degree of activity as requisite to success in so hazardous and so difficult a feat. It is my design to show you, first, that the thing might possibly have been accomplished: but, secondly and *chiefly*, I wish to impress upon your understanding the *very extraordinary*—the almost preternatural character of that agility which could have accomplished it.

'You will say, no doubt, using the language of the law, that "to make out my case" I should rather undervalue than insist upon a full estimation of the activity required in this matter. This may be the practice in law, but it is not the usage of reason. My ultimate object is only the truth. My immediate purpose is to lead you to place in juxtaposition that *very unusual* activity of which I have just spoken with that *very peculiar* shrill (or harsh) and *unequal* voice, about whose nationality no two persons could be found to agree, and in whose utterance no syllabification could be detected.'

At these words a vague and half-formed conception of the meaning of Dupin flitted over my mind. I seemed to be upon the verge of comprehension without power to comprehend—men, at times, find themselves upon the brink of remembrance without being able, in the end, to remember. My friend went on with his discourse.

'You will see,' he said, 'that I have shifted the question from the mode of egress to that of ingress. It was my design to convey the idea that both were effected in the same manner, at the same point. Let us now revert to the interior of the room. Let us survey the appearances here. The drawers of the bureau, it is said, had been rifled, although many articles of apparel still remained within them. The conclusion here is absurd. It is a mere guess—a very silly one—and no more. How are we to know that the articles found in the drawers were not all these drawers had originally contained? Madame L'Espanaye and her daughter lived an exceedingly retired life—saw no company—seldom went out—had little use for numerous changes of habiliment. Those found were at least of as good quality as any likely to be possessed by these ladies. If a thief had taken any, why did he not take the best—why did he not take all? In a word, why did he abandon four thousand francs in gold to encumber himself with a bundle of linen? The gold *was* abandoned. Nearly the whole sum mentioned by Monsieur Mignaud, the banker, was discovered, in bags, upon the floor. I wish you, therefore, to discard from your thoughts the blundering idea of *motive*, engendered in the brains of the police by that portion of the evidence which speaks of money delivered at the door of the house. Coincidences ten times as remarkable as this (the delivery of the money, and murder committed within three days upon the party receiving it) happen to all of us every hour of our lives, without attracting even momentary notice. Coincidences, in general, are great stumbling-blocks in the way of that class of thinkers who have been educated to know nothing of the theory of probabilities—that theory to which the most glorious objects of human research are indebted for the most glorious of illustration. In the present instance, had the gold been gone, the fact of its delivery three days before would have formed something more than a coincidence. It would have been corroborative of this idea of motive. But, under the real circumstances of the case, if we are to suppose gold the motive of this outrage, we must also imagine the perpetrator so vacillating an idiot as to have abandoned his gold and his motive together.

'Keeping now steadily in mind the points to which I have drawn your attention—that peculiar voice, that unusual agility, and that startling absence of motive in a murder so singularly atrocious as this—let us glance at the butchery itself. Here is a woman strangled to death by manual strength and thrust up a chimney, head downward. Ordinary assassins employ no such modes of murder as this. Least of all, do they thus dispose of the murdered. In the manner of thrusting the corpse up the chimney, you will admit that there was something *excessively outré*—something altogether irreconcilable with our common notions of human action, even when we suppose the actors the most depraved of men. Think, too, how great must have been that strength which could have thrust the body *up* such an aperture so forcibly that the united vigour of several persons was found barely sufficient to drag it *down!*

'Turn, now, to other indications of the employment of a vigour most marvellous. On the hearth were thick tresses—very thick tresses—of grey human hair. These had been torn out by the roots. You are aware of the great force necessary in tearing thus from the head even twenty or thirty hairs together. You saw the locks in question as well as myself. Their roots (a hideous sight!) were clotted with fragments of the flesh of the scalp—sure token of the prodigious power which had been exerted in uprooting perhaps half a million hairs at a time. The throat of the old lady was not merely cut, but the head absolutely severed from the body: the instrument was a mere razor. I wish you also to look at the *brutal* ferocity of these deeds. Of the bruises upon the body of Madame L'Espanaye I do not speak. Monsieur Dumas, and his worthy coadjutor Monsieur Etienne, have pronounced that they were inflicted by some obtuse instrument; and so far these gentlemen are very correct. The obtuse instrument was clearly the stone pavement in the yard, upon which the victim had fallen from the window which looked in upon the bed. This idea, however simple it may now seem, escaped the police for the same reason that the breadth of the shutters escaped them—because, by the affair of the nails, their perceptions had been hermetically sealed against the possibility of the windows having ever been opened at all.

'If now, in addition to all these things, you have properly reflected upon the odd disorder of the chamber, we have gone so far as to combine the ideas of an agility astounding, a strength superhuman, a ferocity brutal, a butchery without motive, a *grotesquerie* in horror absolutely alien from humanity, and a voice foreign in tone to the ears of men of many nations, and devoid of all distinct or intelligible syllabification. What result, then, has ensued? What impression have I made upon your fancy?'

I felt a creeping of the flesh as Dupin asked me the question. 'A madman,' I said, 'has done this deed—some raving maniac, escaped from a neighbouring *Maison de Santé*.'

'In some respects,' he replied, 'your idea is not irrelevant. But the voices of madmen, even in their wildest paroxysms, are never found to tally with that peculiar voice heard upon the stairs. Madmen are of some nation, and their language, however incoherent in its words, has always the coherence of syllabification. Besides, the hair of a madman is not such as I now hold in my hand. I disentangled this little tuft from the rigidly clutched fingers of Madame L'Espanaye. Tell me what you can make of it.'

'Dupin!' I said, completely unnerved; 'this hair is most unusual—this is no *human* hair.'

'I have not asserted that it is,' said he; 'but, before we decide this point, I wish you to glance at the little sketch I have here traced upon this paper. It is a *facsimile* drawing of what has been described in one portion of the testimony as "dark bruises, and deep indentations of fingernails" upon the throat of Mademoiselle L'Espanaye, and in another (by Messrs Dumas and Etienne) as a "series of livid spots, evidently the impression of fingers".

'You will perceive,' continued my friend, spreading out the paper upon the table before us, 'that this drawing gives the idea of a firm and fixed hold. There is no *slipping* apparent. Each finger has retained—possibly until the death of the victim—the fearful grasp by which it originally embedded itself. Attempt, now, to place all your fingers, at the same time, in the respective impressions as you see them.'

I made the attempt in vain.

'We are possibly not giving this matter a fair trial,' he said. 'The paper is spread out upon a plane surface; but the human throat is cylindrical. Here is a billet of wood, the circumference of which is about that of the throat. Wrap the drawing around it, and try the experiment again.'

I did so; but the difficulty was even more obvious than before. 'This,' I said, 'is the mark of no human hand.'

'Read now,' replied Dupin, 'this passage from Cuvier.'

It was a minute anatomical and generally descriptive account of the large fulvous Ourang-outang of the East Indian Islands. The gigantic stature, the prodigious strength and activity, the wild ferocity, and the imitative propensities of these mammalia are sufficiently well known to all. I understood the full horrors of the murder at once.

'The description of the digits,' said I, as I made an end of reading, 'is in exact accordance with this drawing. I see that no animal but an Ourang-outang, of the species here mentioned, could have impressed the indentations as you have traced them. This tuft of tawny hair, too, is identical in character with that of the beast of Cuvier. But I cannot possibly comprehend the particulars of this frightful mystery. Besides, there were *two* voices heard in contention, and one of them was unquestionably the voice of a Frenchman.'

'True; and you will remember an expression attributed almost unanimously, by the evidence, to this voice—the expression "*mon Dieu!*" This, under the circumstances, has been justly characterized by one of the witnesses (Montani, the confectioner) as an expression of remonstrance or expostulation. Upon these two words, therefore, I have mainly built my hopes of a full solution of the riddle. A Frenchman was cognizant of the murder. It is possible—indeed it is far more than probable—that he was innocent of all participation in the bloody transactions which took place. The Ourang-outang may have escaped from him. He may have traced it to the chamber; but, under the agitating circumstances which ensued, he could never have re-captured it. It is still at large. I will not pursue these guesses—for I have no right to call them more—since the shades of reflection upon which they are based are scarcely of sufficient depth to be appreciable by my own intellect, and since I could not pretend to make them intelligible to the understanding of another. We will call them guesses then, and speak of them as such. If the Frenchman in question is indeed, as I suppose, innocent of this atrocity, this advertisement which I left last night, upon our return home, at the office of *Le Monde* (a paper devoted to the shipping interest, and much sought by sailors), will bring him to our residence.'

He handed me a paper, and I read thus:

CAUGHT—*In the Bois de Boulogne, early in the morning of the — inst.* [the morning of the murder], *a very large, tawny Ourang-outang of the Bornese species. The owner (who is ascertained to be a sailor, belonging to a Maltese vessel) may have the animal again, upon identifying it satisfactorily, and paying a few charges arising from its capture and keeping. Call at No.—, Rue —, Faubourg St Germain—au troisième.*

'How was it possible,' I asked, 'that you should know the man to be a sailor, and belonging to a Maltese vessel?'

'I do *not* know it,' said Dupin. 'I am not *sure* of it. Here, however, is a small piece of ribbon, which from its form, and from its greasy appearance, has evidently been used in tying the hair in one of those long *queues* of which sailors are so fond. Moreover, this knot is one which few besides sailors can tie, and is peculiar to the Maltese. I picked the ribbon up at the foot of the lightning-rod. It could not have belonged to either of the deceased. Now if, after all, I am wrong in my induction from this ribbon, that the Frenchman was a sailor belonging to a Maltese vessel, still I can have done no harm in saying what I did in the advertisement. If I am in error, he will merely suppose that I have been misled by some circumstance into which he will not take the trouble to inquire. But if I am right, a great point is gained. Cognizant although innocent of the murder, the Frenchman will naturally hesitate about replying to the advertisement—about demanding the Ourang-outang. He will reason thus: "I am innocent; I am poor; my Ourang-outang is of great value—to one in my circumstances a fortune of itself—why should I lose it through idle apprehensions of danger? Here it is, within my grasp. It was found in the Bois de Boulogne—at a vast distance from the scene of that butchery. How can it ever be suspected that a brute beast should have done the deed? The police are at fault—they have failed to procure the slightest clew. Should they even trace the animal, it would be impossible to prove me cognizant of the murder, or to implicate me in guilt on account of that cognizance. Above all, *I am known.* The advertiser designates me as the possessor of the beast. I am not sure to what limit his knowledge may extend. Should I avoid claiming a property of so great value, which it is known that I possess, I will render the animal at least liable to suspicion. It is not my policy to attract attention either to myself or to the beast. I will answer the advertisement, get the Ourang-outang, and keep it close until this matter has blown over.'"

At this moment we heard a step upon the stairs.

'Be ready,' said Dupin, 'with your pistols, but neither use them nor show them until at a signal from myself.'

The front door of the house had been left open, and the visitor had entered, without ringing, and advanced several steps upon the staircase. Now, however, he seemed to hesitate. Presently we heard him descending. Dupin was moving quickly to the door, when we again heard him coming up. He did not turn back a second time, but stepped up with decision, and rapped at the door of our chamber.

'Come in,' said Dupin, in a cheerful and hearty tone.

A man entered. He was a sailor, evidently—a tall, stout, and muscular-looking person, with a certain daredevil expression of countenance, not altogether unprepossessing. His face, greatly sunburnt, was more than half hidden by whisker and *mustachio.* He had with him a huge oaken cudgel, but appeared to be otherwise unarmed. He bowed awkwardly, and bade us 'good evening' in French accents, which, although somewhat Neufchatelish, were still sufficiently indicative of a Parisian origin.

'Sit down, my friend,' said Dupin. 'I suppose you have called about the Ourang-outang. Upon my word, I almost envy you the possession of him; a remarkably fine and no doubt a very valuable animal. How old do you suppose him to be?'

The sailor drew a long breath, with the air of a man relieved of some intolerable burden, and then replied, in an assured tone:

'I have no way of telling—but he can't be more than four or five years old. Have you got him here?'

'Oh no, we had no conveniences for keeping him here. He is at a livery stable in the Rue Dubourg, just by. You can get him in the morning. Of course you are prepared to identify the property?'

'To be sure I am, sir.'

'I shall be sorry to part with him,' said Dupin.

'I don't mean that you should be at all this trouble for nothing, sir,' said the man. 'Couldn't expect it. Am very willing to pay a reward for the finding of the animal—that is to say, anything in reason.'

'Well,' replied my friend, 'that is all very fair, to be sure. Let me think!—what should I have? Oh! I will tell you. My reward shall be this. You shall give me all the information in your power about these murders in the Rue Morgue.'

Dupin said the last words in a very low tone, and very quietly. Just as quietly, too, he walked toward the door, locked it and put the key in his pocket. He then drew a pistol from his bosom and placed it, without the least flurry, upon the table.

The sailor's face flushed up as if he were struggling with suffocation. He started to his feet and grasped his cudgel, but the next moment he fell back into his seat, trembling violently, and with the countenance of death itself. He spoke not a word. I pitied him from the bottom of my heart.

'My friend,' said Dupin, in a kind tone, 'you are alarming yourself unnecessarily—you are indeed. We mean you no harm whatever. I pledge you the honour of a gentleman, and of a Frenchman, that we intend you no injury. I perfectly well know that you are innocent of the atrocities in the Rue Morgue. It will not do, however, to deny that you are in some measure implicated in them. From what I have already said, you must know that I have had means of information about this matter—means of which you could never have dreamed. Now the thing stands thus. You have done nothing which you could have avoided—nothing, certainly, which renders you culpable. You were not even guilty of robbery, when you might have robbed with impunity. You have nothing to conceal. You have no reason for concealment. On the other hand, you are bound by every principle of honour to confess all you know. An innocent man is now imprisoned, charged with that crime of which you can point out the perpetrator.'

The sailor had recovered his presence of mind, in a great measure, while Dupin uttered these words; but his original boldness of bearing was all gone.

'So help me God,' said he, after a brief pause, 'I will tell you all I know about this affair; but I do not expect you to believe one half I say—I would be a fool indeed if I did. Still, I am innocent, and I will make a clean breast if I die for it.'

What he stated was, in substance, this. He had lately made a voyage to the Indian Archipelago. A party, of which he formed one, landed at Borneo, and passed into the interior on an excursion of pleasure. Himself and a companion had captured the Ourang-outang. This companion dying, the animal fell into his own exclusive possession. After great trouble, occasioned by the intractable ferocity of his captive during the home voyage, he at length succeeded in lodging it safely at his own residence in Paris, where, not to attract towards himself the unpleasant curiosity of his neighbours, he kept it carefully secluded, until such time as it should recover from a wound in the foot, received from a splinter on board ship. His ultimate design was to sell it.

Returning home from some sailors' frolic the night, or rather in the morning, of the murder, he found the beast occupying his own bedroom, into which it had broken from a closet adjoining, where it had been, as was thought, securely confined. Razor in hand, and fully lathered, it was sitting before a looking-glass, attempting the operation of shaving, in which it had no doubt previously watched its master through the key-hole of the closet. Terrified at the sight of so dangerous a weapon in the possession of an animal so ferocious, and so well able to use it, the man, for some moments, was at a loss what to do. He had been accustomed, however, to quiet the creature, even in its fiercest moods, by the use of a whip, and to this he now resorted. Upon sight of it, the Ourang-outang sprang at once through the door of the chamber, down the stairs, and thence, through a window unfortunately open, into the street.

The Frenchman followed in despair; the ape, razor still in hand, occasionally stopping to look back and gesticulate at its pursuer, until the latter had nearly come up with it. It then again made off. In this manner the chase continued for a long time. The streets were profoundly quiet, as it was nearly three o'clock in the morning. In passing down an alley in the rear of the Rue Morgue, the fugitive's attention was arrested by a light gleaming from the open window of Madame L'Espanaye's chamber, in the fourth storey of her house. Rushing to the building, it perceived the lightning rod, clambered up with inconceivable agility, grasped the shutter, which was thrown fully back against the wall, and, by its means, swung itself directly upon the headboard of the bed. The whole feat did not occupy a minute. The shutter was kicked open again by the Ourang-outang as it entered the room.

The sailor, in the meantime, was both rejoiced and perplexed. He had strong hopes of now recapturing the brute, as it could scarcely escape from the trap into which it had ventured, except by the rod, where it might be intercepted as it came down. On the other hand, there was much cause for anxiety as to what it might do in the house. This latter reflection urged the man still to follow the fugitive. A lightning rod is ascended without difficulty, especially by a sailor; but, when he had arrived as high as the window, which lay far to his left, his career was stopped; the most that he could accomplish was to reach over so as to obtain a glimpse of the interior of the room. At this glimpse he nearly fell from his hold through excess of horror. Now it was that those hideous shrieks arose upon the night, which had startled from slumber the inmates of the Rue Morgue. Madame L'Espanaye and her daughter, habited in their night clothes, had apparently been occupied in arranging some papers in the iron chest already mentioned, which had been wheeled into the middle of the room. It was open, and its contents lay beside it on the floor. The victims must have been sitting with their backs toward the window; and, from the time elapsing between the ingress of the beast and the screams, it seems probable that it was not immediately perceived. The flapping-to of the shutter would naturally have been attributed to the wind.

As the sailor looked in, the gigantic animal had seized Madame L'Espanaye by the hair (which was loose, as she had been combing it) and was flourishing the razor about her face, in imitation of the motions of a barber. The daughter lay prostrate and motionless; she had swooned. The screams and struggles of the old lady (during which the hair was torn from her head) had the effect of changing the probably pacific purposes of the Ourang-outang into those of wrath. With one determined sweep of its muscular arm it nearly severed her head from her body. The sight of blood inflamed its anger into frenzy. Gnashing its teeth, and flashing fire from its eyes, it flew upon the body of the girl, and embedded its fearful talons in her throat, retaining its grasp until she expired. Its wandering and wild glances fell at this moment upon the head of the bed, over which the face of its master, rigid with horror, was just discernible. The fury of the beast, who no doubt bore still in mind the dreaded whip, was instantly converted into fear. Conscious of having deserved punishment, it seemed desirous of concealing its bloody deeds, and skipped about the chamber in an agony of nervous agitation; throwing down and breaking the furniture as it moved, and dragging the bed from the bedstead. In conclusion, it seized first the corpse of the daughter, and thrust it up the chimney, as it was found; then that of the old lady, which it immediately hurled through the window headlong.

As the ape approached the casement with its mutilated burden, the sailor shrank aghast to the rod, and, rather gliding than clambering down it, hurried at once home—dreading the consequences of the butchery, and gladly abandoning in his terror all solicitude about the fate of the Ourang-outang. The words heard by the party upon the staircase were the Frenchman's exclamations of horror and affright, commingled with the fiendish jabberings of the brute.

I have scarcely anything to add. The Ourang-outang must have escaped from the chamber, by the rod, just before the break of the door. It must have closed the window as it passed through it. It was subsequently caught by the owner himself, who obtained for it a very large sum at the *Jardin des Plantes*. Le Bon was instantly released, upon our narration of the circumstances (with some comments from Dupin) at the bureau of the Prefect of Police. This functionary, however well-disposed to my friend, could not altogether conceal his chagrin at the turn which affairs had taken, and was fain to indulge in a sarcasm or two about the propriety of every person minding his own business.

'Let him talk,' said Dupin, who had not thought it necessary to reply. 'Let him discourse; it will ease his conscience. I am satisfied with having defeated him in his own castle. Nevertheless, that he failed in the solution of this mystery is by no means that matter for wonder which he supposes it; for, in truth, our friend the Prefect is somewhat too cunning to be profound. In his wisdom is no *stamen*. It is all head and no body, like the pictures of the Goddess Laverna—or, at best, all head and shoulders, like a codfish. But he is a good creature after all. I like him especially for one master stroke of cant, by which he has attained his reputation for ingenuity. I mean the way he has "*de nier ce qui est, et d'expliquer ce qui n'est pas*".*

THE END

---

* 'To deny what is, and to explain what is not' (from *Nouvelle Heloise* by Jean-Jacques Rousseau, 1761).